He spun her around and, to her surprise, began buttoning her coat.

"I can do it," Tahlia said, halting his hands with her own.

"I want to make sure you're warm," Maximus said, brushing her hands aside as he continued his task.

Tahlia looked down. Didn't he know she was not only warm, but she was also on fire from his touch? She hadn't recovered from his earlier kiss, and being in this confined space with Maximus was playing havoc on her senses. Her heart was already beating an erratic rhythm.

"Tahlia, look at me," Maximus's voice was husky with desire.

She met his eyes with hers, and they scanned her face slowly and seductively. And when his gaze slid downward to her lips and he lifted his thumb to caress them, her pulse quickened. Maximus tilted her chin upward with a finger to inch her closer to him. Tahlia knew what was coming next, and there was no hesitation on her part. She twined her fingers into his curly hair at the back of his head as she'd been longing to do. Sweet relief flooded her as he hauled her against him, bent his head and closed his mouth over hers.

Dear Reader,

I hope you find Maximus Knight's story a satisfying conclusion to the Knights of Los Angeles series that began with *Taming Her Tycoon*. My idea of a sibling rivalry over the family dynasty came from watching the television show *Empire*.

I love the arc of each character's metamorphosis. Maximus can't get past his father's betrayal in giving half his birthright to his brother, Lucius Knight, with Tahlia Armstrong as the tiebreaker vote. Maximus is equal parts charmer and schemer as he tries to retain his empire by seducing lovable Tahlia. She becomes empathetic to Maximus's plight after realizing her surrogate father, Arthur Knight, had faults. It's exciting to see Maximus's growth as he falls for Tahlia's sweet nature and accepts his new brother.

My next book, *His San Diego Sweetheart*, debuts in spring 2018. Visit my website, www.yahrahstjohn.com, or write me at yahrah@yahrahstjohn.com for details.

Yahrah St. John

Taming
HER
Billionaire

YAHRAH ST. JOHN

HARLEQUIN® KIMANI™ ROMANCE

Recycling programs
for this product may
not exist in your area.

ISBN-13: 978-0-373-86521-5

Taming Her Billionaire

For questions and comments about the quality of this book please contact us
at CustomerService@Harlequin.com.

H HARLEQUIN®
www.Harlequin.com

Printed in U.S.A.

Yahrah St. John is the author of twenty-five books, seventeen with the Harlequin Kimani Romance line. When she's not at home crafting one of her sexy romances with compelling heroes, feisty heroines and a dash of family drama, she can be found in the kitchen cooking one of her gourmet meals discovered on the Food Network for her husband. Or this thrill-seeking junkie can be found traveling the globe seeking out her next adventure. A graduate of Hyde Park Career Academy, she earned a bachelor of arts degree in English from Northwestern University. St. John is a member of Romance Writers of America but is an avid reader of all genres. She lives in sunny Orlando, the City Beautiful, where there's great weather all year round. For more information, please visit www.yahrahstjohn.com.

Books by Yahrah St. John

Harlequin Kimani Romance

Two to Tango
Need You Now
Lost Without You
Formula for Passion
Delicious Destiny
A Chance with You
Heat Wave of Desire
Cappuccino Kisses
Taming Her Tycoon
Miami After Hours
Taming Her Billionaire

Visit the Author Profile page
at Harlequin.com for more titles.

To my husband, Freddie Blackman—
you light up my life.

Chapter 1

Maximus Xavier Knight stared at the beautiful woman who'd just entered the library of his family's estate for the reading of his father Arthur Knight's will. Had she really just said she was his partner? Was he in some alternative universe? Surely his father's attorncy, Robert Kellogg, hadn't just informed him that his father had bestowed 49 percent equally to him and his illegitimate older brother, Lucius Knight, and given this random yet stunning woman the remaining 2 percent?

One thing was for sure, she was a knockout. His cyes skimmed over her. The wrap dress she wore clung to her shapely curves, showing him she had generous breasts and hips he could grab on to and legs that went on for miles. Long, flowing black hair hung down her back in soft luxurious waves. Her smooth tapioca-colored skin looked soft to the touch. He drank in every detail, her high cheekbones, finely arched eyebrows and full kissable lips, which held a hint of pink lipstick. Her expressive large brown eyes were mascara-coated and looking at him intently.

"Maximus, I presume." She held out her hand. "Tahlia, Tahlia Armstrong."

Maximus extended his hand, cupping her small, soft one in his, and shook it. The brief contact sent an arc of desire shooting straight through him. They stared at one another for several beats before she lowered her hand, making Maximus wonder if he'd imagined the electric connection.

"Ms. Armstrong, welcome," Robert said. "I was hoping you would have come earlier."

"Sorry." Tahlia blushed. "Promptness isn't my strong suit." She found an empty chair beside his half brother, Lucius, and took a seat. She was clearly embarrassed by her tardiness but seemed to have known more than any of them did.

"Omigod!" Maximus's mother, Charlotte, cried into her handkerchief by his side. He knew she must be in shock just as he was by his father's bequest, but he was determined not to show weakness.

"Robert." Maximus remained standing and walked over to his father's longtime friend. "Is this will iron-clad?"

The attorney frowned. "Meaning was your father of sound mind when he wrote it?"

"Of course he was," Lucius's mother, Jocelyn Turner, burst aloud, jumping out of her seat. "This was his way of finally acknowledging Lucius." She pointed to her son, who was still seated next to his fiancée, Naomi Brooks.

"You have no say here." Charlotte Knight stopped sniffing long enough to speak and rise from her seat to face her nemesis. "Arthur was my husband, not yours. You were nothing more than his low-rate mistress, one he couldn't bother to be seen with."

"Mother! That's enough." Maximus didn't want an all-out brawl to break out. Lucius had stood as well and stepped in front of his mother in full protective mode.

"Everyone, please," Robert spoke loudly, interrupting the crowd. "I need you all to take your seats."

Reluctantly, both mothers sat down while Maximus and Lucius remained standing. Maximus didn't know what to make of his older brother, but he knew he'd be a formidable opponent. He was six foot two with a square jaw and an athletic physique. Even though he worked out often, Maximus wasn't sure he could take him down physically, but there were other ways.

"Why would he do this?" Lucius asked, turning to Robert. "I know nothing about the shipping business, and I want no part of any inheritance Arthur Knight may have left for me."

"Good." Max smiled. He was glad to see that he and his brother were on the same page. He didn't need or want Lucius around, and apparently he felt the same way. "It's settled. You can sign over your shares and we can be done with this business."

"No!" Tahlia's voice rang out. "It's not what your father wanted."

Maximus spun around on his heel. The withering look he gave her may have frightened many an employee in his office, but not Tahlia. He guessed she was somewhere in the neighborhood of five foot nine or ten, and wasn't backing down from him even though he stood several inches taller. "And how would you know what my father wanted?"

"I'd like to know the answer to that question, as well," his mother said. Fury was etched across her face. How was it that she was in the dark about yet another woman in his father's life?

"Because he talked to me about his failure to do the right thing by his sons," Tahlia responded.

So she knew about Lucius? How long? Was she another one of his father's mistresses? She was young and incredibly beautiful. How had she gotten herself mixed up with an older married man when she could have her pick of men? A million questions scrambled Maximus's brain, but before he could fire them at her, Robert interjected.

"Everyone, I know Arthur's wishes must come as a shock to all of you," Robert stated, "but I can assure you he was of sound mind and body when he wrote this will. Further, as Ms. Armstrong has stated, it was Arthur's hope that you both could work together side by side and truly become brothers."

"Robert, you act like this is some kind of family reunion," Maximus returned, "when that's far from the case. We—" he motioned around the room "—are here because my father was a liar, a cheat and a coward. It sickens me. And only now in his death does he have the courage to speak up? This is nothing short of Shakespearean."

"Please, take some time to let all of this sink in, give it time to settle," Robert replied softly. "You'll see he was *finally* trying to be fair."

"While ripping the ground right out from underneath me? He's given a complete stranger—" Maximus responded with contempt as he pointed to Tahlia "—two percent of his company, and I want to know why."

"I don't know why," Tahlia replied, squaring her shoulders. "I certainly didn't ask him for it. I was just a friend. An ear to listen when he needed it. And vice versa. I know that may be hard or strange to believe given our age difference, but nothing untoward happened between me and Arthur. He was like a father to me, giving me advice about life, work…and I—I miss him, too…" Her voice broke, and she turned away from him, clutching her hand to her mouth.

It made Maximus feel like a heel because he'd clearly upset her when he hadn't meant to. He just wanted answers. He had a right to know why half of the company he'd devoted his life to had been given to a son his father never claimed and someone who wasn't even a member of the Knight family. He was boiling with rage, but venting at a woman wasn't his style. Nor would he give Lucius the satisfaction of seeing him falter, but one thing was for certain: he wasn't about to give up the battle for Tahlia's 2 percent, which was rightfully his.

Maximus bent down to speak to his mother, who was still reeling at the news. He whispered in her ear, trying to soothe her frayed nerves. "There's nothing we can do at this moment. Give me some time to figure this out, okay?"

She nodded.

Maximus glanced up and watched Robert pack up his briefcase and then come over to him. "Max, I'm sorry how this all turned out for you," he said. "I warned Arthur that this wasn't the best approach, and he should have discussed his choices with you sooner rather than blindsiding you."

Maximus shrugged. "Why should I be surprised, Robert? I've never been able to do enough or achieve enough to gain my father's respect, and now this? He didn't even think I could run his company."

Robert patted his shoulder reassuringly and quietly walked away.

What was he supposed to do now? Maximus's mind was jumbled as to what his next move should be. He glanced across the room and saw Lucius, Jocelyn and Naomi speaking quietly while Tahlia stood in the background, watching the entire scene. She was clearly uncomfortable to be in the middle of a family squabble. And it surprised him that he felt protective over a woman he'd just met and wanted to comfort her, but he did.

So he strolled toward her.

She smiled when he approached, and Maximus's stomach flipped. Something that never happened with other women. Usually his time spent with the fairer sex was either as a companion for an event or his bedmate. Nothing more.

Tahlia Armstrong fit neither of those categories.

"Are you all right?" he inquired.

"Shouldn't I be asking you that question?" she responded with a half smile. "I mean, I didn't have my entire life turned upside down today with no warning."

"Very true, but you also became an instant millionaire today," he said smoothly, regarding her intently. "Two percent in Knight Shipping is nothing to laugh at."

"No, I don't suppose it is," she said demurely.

And then there it was again, a hint of a blush on her rosy cheeks. She looked downward, not quite looking at him, and that was when he realized Tahlia Armstrong was flustered by him. Maximus had to figure out how to use that to his advantage.

"You should stay for dinner," he stated quietly, surprising even himself with the offer.

"D-dinner?"

He grinned. "Yes, you do eat, don't you?"

She chuckled, and Maximus had to admit he liked the sound of it. "I do."

"Then join me. I mean, me and my mother that is."

Tahlia glanced over to his brother. "Is Lucius and his family welcome to join us?"

Max bristled inwardly. He hated being backed into a corner, but in order to figure out his next move where Tahlia was concerned, he might have to tolerate a meal with his older brother and harlot of a mother. Though he had no ill will against Naomi.

"If that means you'll agree, then yes."

Tahlia smiled. She'd won a small victory in getting Maximus to agree to dinner with his brother, Lucius. When Robert had first telephoned her a couple of days ago, she'd been unprepared for the bombshell he was about to drop on her. One day she was a lowly assistant at an art gallery in Los Angeles, the next she was the owner of the gallery as well as a 2 percent partner in Knight Shipping, one of the largest shipping companies in the United States. Talk about a change in circumstances overnight! Not to mention she was finally going to get close enough to Maximus to actually have a conversation after seeing him only from afar!

Tahlia had been so shocked by the turn of events, she'd kept the news to herself and hadn't even told her mother, Sophia, or sister, Kaitlynn. How could she tell them she was tied indefinitely to the Knights and Maximus, the man she'd secretly crushed on the last year? Ever since she'd first seen him from across the room at one of the gallery's exhibit openings, he'd been on her mind. Not that he had noticed her that night. When she'd asked Robert why he was telling her in advance of Arthur's bequest, Robert indicated he thought there might trouble between the two brothers when they learned their fate and was hoping she'd play peacemaker.

It was a tall order, one which she knew wouldn't be

achieved overnight, but it was a start. They were family after all. And for some reason, Arthur, her dear friend, had chosen her to lead the effort, and Tahlia was determined not to let him down.

Tahlia tried not to show nerves as she and Maximus walked over toward Lucius and his family, but instantly a chill spiked in the air.

"Lucius." Maximus nodded in his direction.

"Max." Lucius used his youngest brother's nickname, and Tahlia felt Maximus immediately tense beside her. She was sure it was used only by family and close friends, certainly not a brother he'd known nothing about until a couple of weeks ago.

Tahlia had been horrified when she'd heard that Arthur had been caught in flagrante with Lucius's mother, Jocelyn, in a hotel room and had a heart attack. The news media had been unforgiving in their portrayal of the shipping magnate and his womanizing ways. And when the press had realized that Lucius was the product of their decades-long affair, they'd been brutal. It was no wonder both men were angry. They had a right to be. Arthur should have been honest with them much sooner.

"I've invited Ms. Armstrong," Maximus began, but she interrupted him.

"Tahlia."

Maximus nodded. "I've invited Tahlia to dinner this evening. And she thought you and your lovely fiancée might like to join us."

Tahlia frowned. She was sure she'd said Lucius's family, including his mother, but was that asking too much under the circumstances?

"That's quite generous of you, Max," Lucius replied with a wide grin. "And I'll stay if my mother is welcome."

Lucius was purposely baiting him, and Tahlia hated that she was the cause, but Maximus didn't seem fazed—or at least not that he was showing outwardly. In Tahlia's opinion, he plastered a fake smile on his face before saying, "I suppose, but it might be best to keep both our mothers on opposite sides of the table."

"That would be prudent," Lucius responded.

Soon they were all headed in the direction of the dining room. Tahlia was shocked when Maximus returned to her side after briefly speaking with his mother. She could see Charlotte Knight recoil with the turn of events as evidenced by the glare she threw in Tahlia's direction, but she remained silent and did as Maximus instructed.

Once they made it to the beautifully appointed dining area, Charlotte immediately sat at the head of the table, making it clear this was her home and they were all just visitors in it. Maximus flanked his mother to the left, leaving the seat to her right open, which Tahlia reluctantly took. Meanwhile, Lucius and his mother sat beside Tahlia while his fiancée sat next to Maximus.

A uniformed man Tahlia could only assume was the butler came to speak with Mrs. Knight. Several seconds later waitstaff entered to fill their water glasses as well as offer them wine with their meal. Other than everyone selecting their choice of red or white, the silence in the room was deafening.

"Th-thank you for having us," Tahlia offered, glancing at Charlotte. "It's really quite generous."

"Did we have much choice?" Mrs. Knight queried under her breath.

"If you don't want us here, we can leave," Lucius responded tightly from across the table, and Tahlia could feel the tension ratchet up a notch, but Maximus intervened.

"We've invited you and you're our guest," Maximus stated wanly. He turned to the company on his side. "Naomi Brooks—" he offered her his hand "—it's a pleasure to finally meet you. I've heard quite a lot about Brooks & Johnson. I believe you use their products don't you, Mother?"

He turned to Charlotte.

She gave the first sincere smile Tahlia had seen since she'd arrived. "Yes, I do. They are the only products my salon carries where I get my facials." She lightly touched her cheek. "They're really quite remarkable products."

"Thank you." Naomi smiled.

"You started the company with your best friend, yes?" Maximus inquired, sipping his wine and leaning back in his chair to regard her.

"Yes, in our apartment in college," Naomi replied.

"And turned it into a billion-dollar business," Maximus added. "You've got yourself quite a find here, big brother."

Tahlia gave Lucius a sideward glance. The love in his eyes was evident as he grinned across the table at his fiancée.

"And you?" Charlotte turned her attention to Tahlia. "What is it that you do, dear?"

"Mother," Maximus cautioned. The tone in his voice told her to tread lightly.

"I'm just being cordial," she replied, reaching for her wineglass.

"Up until recently, I worked as an assistant at Art Gallery Twenty-One."

"That was one of Father's favorite galleries," Maximus said, offering Tahlia a warm smile.

"Have circumstances changed?" Charlotte asked.

"As a matter of fact they have," Tahlia answered. "Robert informed me that Arthur was owner of the gallery and has bequeathed it to me."

A loud gasp escaped from Charlotte, but she soon recovered. "So now you own it? You must have made quite the impression on my husband." She took another sip of her red wine. "Very much like other people I know."

Her implication was clear that Arthur and Tahlia had an intimate relationship, a seedy one. Fury boiled inside Tahlia, but she needn't have worried because Jocelyn rose to the bait.

"If you're insinuating something, Charlotte," Jocelyn spoke after being silent since they were seated, "just say it. Maybe then we can all end this whole charade."

Tahlia suspected it must be very difficult for Jocelyn to sit in her former lover's home with his wife and son, knowing she'd had an affair with the man for years and produced a child. A child who was sitting beside her but had never been acknowledged, until now.

"Au contraire, contraire," Charlotte replied with a snort. "It gives me great pleasure to sit with the mistress of my lying, cheating excuse for a husband and her illegitimate offspring after you've in essence ripped *my* child's inheritance right out of his hands."

"I did no such thing!" Lucius roared from beside her. His dark eyes blazed with indignation. "I didn't ask for any of this. Neither did he." He flung his hands in Maximus's direction. "Did you know Arthur was cheating on your mother?"

Maximus glared at him, and at first Tahlia thought

he wouldn't respond, but then he shook his head. "Of course I didn't," he finally replied. His dark brown eyes were very much like Lucius's. "Do you think if I did I would have let Arthur continue to humiliate my mother with yours?"

Tahlia tried to speak. "Everyone, why don't we calm down. I think dinner is coming." Or at least the salads were. Several waitstaff entered the room carrying plates filled with mixed greens, cranberries and walnuts and what appeared to be some sort of vinaigrette. As they set a plate in front of her, Tahlia couldn't wait to dig in.

Maximus gave her a small smile from across the table, but it was pointless because Jocelyn rose to her feet. "I'm sorry, Lucius." She turned to her son. "I can't sit here and break bread with these people in A-Arthur's home. It's just too much." Seconds later, she pushed her chair back and rushed out of the dining room.

"Good riddance!" Charlotte said with a smile.

"That was uncalled for, Mother," Maximus hissed. "Apologize."

"For what? For speaking the truth in my *own* home?" she replied bitterly.

Lucius rose from his chair beside Tahlia, and she watched in horror as Naomi did the same. Despite her best efforts to bridge the gap between the brothers, it was all in vain.

"We're leaving," Lucius stated, throwing his napkin onto the table.

"You don't have to go." Tahlia attempted to save the day.

Lucius patted her on the shoulder, preventing her from getting up. Then he bent down and whispered in her ear. "Good try, ole girl, but you're going to have to do a lot better than this to get us to become a family.

C'mon, Naomi." He extended his hand to his fiancée and headed for the door.

Maximus stood as well, buttoning his suit jacket that looked sexy as hell on him, and strode confidently to the dining room door and met his brother at the exit.

"Lucius." He inclined his head. "I'm sure we'll be speaking soon."

"No doubt," Lucius replied. Seconds later he and Naomi were gone.

"Did you really have to be so gauche?" Maximus asked, turning to his mother after Lucius and his family had gone. It was only the three of them remaining.

"Quite frankly I did." She stood. "You should be happy I was willing to get through salad, given everything that woman—" she pointed to the door Jocelyn Turner had just vacated "—did to me."

"That you *let* them do to you," Maximus corrected. "Don't try to rewrite history."

"I—I'm not going to talk about this right now," Charlotte huffed. She reached for her wineglass and without another word took it along with her as she stormed out of the room.

"Was it something I said?" Tahlia asked when it was just her and Maximus alone in the dining room.

He let out a loud rumble of laughter that was so infectious Tahlia couldn't resist and joined in on the fun. Soon, they were both howling, unable to control themselves. After several moments, the chuckles finally subsided and Maximus came beside her, pulling out the chair next to her that Lucius had vacated.

"That was a complete and utter disaster," he stated unequivocally, leaning back in his chair and staring openly at her.

She nodded her agreement. "It was."

"I applaud you for trying to calm the waters, but considering the circumstances, you must know that this is an untenable situation. We are never going to be a family."

"Who says? There are all sorts of families."

"You're not really that naive are you?" Maximus inquired, peering at Tahlia. Where the hell had she come from anyway? He knew his father liked to frequent the art gallery. And now he knew she was the cause. And could he really blame his father? Tahlia Armstrong was a bombshell.

Had she, too, been carrying on an affair with his father right under their noses? Or at least under his mother's since she'd known for years about his father's affair with Jocelyn Turner. How could she stomach staying in the marriage knowing he was unfaithful?

Maximus would never have tolerated such a betrayal. When he married, *if he married,* his wife would be his and only his. He'd kill the man who dared look at her, let alone touch her. It was why he couldn't understand how his mother allowed the adultery to continue for *decades*.

"I'm not naive," Tahlia responded. "I just choose to be positive and was trying to make the best of the situation."

"Very noble, but wasted on us," Maximus replied, rising to his feet. "Can I walk you out?"

She blinked several times. Perhaps she thought they were still going to continue with dinner. Not tonight. He needed time to think and strategize his next move.

"Uh, yeah, sure," she said.

Maximus pulled her chair out and followed Tahlia as they walked down the corridor. He purposely walked behind her so he could enjoy the view of her backside.

His groin tightened as she swayed, and God help him, he wanted her.

Suddenly she stopped short and turned to him. "In the spirit of keeping the peace, I want to make it clear to you that nothing happened between your father and me."

"And you expect me to believe that?"

Her eyes narrowed. "Yes, I do, because it's the truth. When your father visited the gallery, all we did was sit and talk during his lunch hour. He was a father figure to me, Maximus. Nothing more."

"What on earth would he have to discuss with you?" As soon as he said the words, he knew they sounded harsh. "Listen, I'm sorry, all right? But even you have to see where I'm coming from. A woman I've never met had a relationship with my father that not only did no one know about, but apparently he was more caring with you than he'd ever been with me."

When they made it to the large oak door with a stained glass insert, he held it open for her, and she stepped outside. "I'm sorry. Truly sorry that Arthur wasn't more open with you and that you didn't get to know the man I knew. And th-thank you for dinner." She smiled up at him with her big brown eyes, and Max felt his manhood swell. He'd only just met Tahlia, but she was having a profound effect on him.

"It wasn't much of one, I'm afraid."

"You tried."

"Have a good night." He watched her walk to her car and shut the door. Then he headed directly for the library. He usually loved the room because it was surrounded on three sides by bookshelves up to the crown molding at the ceiling. The furniture was upholstered in rich chocolate-brown leather to match the solid oak desk his father had once used. But Maximus didn't care for any of that tonight and went straight for the wet bar. He poured himself a bourbon straight up. He walked over to the French doors across the room and opened them, staring out over the manicured great lawn. He sipped his drink and thought about his next move.

He hadn't felt such a strong physical pull toward a female in a long time, if ever. Wanting Tahlia Armstrong was irrational and not advisable. He needed to figure out how he could control her and the situation. She now owned the *two* most important percent of shares at Knight Shipping because hers was the deciding vote, thanks to his father's machinations. Had his father done this to spite him because Maximus had suggested taking Knight Shipping public when Arthur was adamantly opposed to it? Had he given Tahlia those shares to ensure it never happened? If so, she was no match for him. Expansion was inevitable, and the board now composed of Lucius and Tahlia would have to vote on it. Maximus would do *whatever* was necessary to ensure he was successful.

He'd seen the way she looked at him today. She wasn't unaffected by him either. He'd noticed earlier that she stammered whenever he came within close proximity to her. Perhaps their mutual attraction could work to his advantage. Sexing her was an intriguing possibility.

Maximus heard a noise behind him and turned to find his mother standing in the doorway. "Care to pour me one of those?" she asked, inclining her head to the drink in his hand. The red wine she'd had earlier was nowhere to be seen.

"Sure." He stepped back into the library and took care of making her a drink. Then he walked over to where she'd made herself comfortable on his father's favorite easy chair and handed her the bourbon.

"Thank you." He settled across from her in another chair, and they were both quiet for a long moment before she finally spoke. "I'm still in shock, Max. I can't believe your father did this to us."

"You mean to me," he responded. "I'm the one he pushed and pushed to be the best at everything. I'm the one he said would run Knight Shipping one day, but instead, he gives half the company to my illegitimate brother? A son he couldn't even acknowledge while he lived? A son who knows nothing about the shipping business? You have no idea what it feels like to be in my shoes, Mother." Maximus threw back the remaining bourbon in his glass and then jumped up and went to the bar for another one.

Maybe, just maybe, he could drown out the hurt and betrayal he felt at a father who'd never loved Maximus as much as he'd loved him.

"I'm so sorry, Max," his mother cried. "I thought I was doing what was best for you."

He spun around on his heel. "By staying with a man who didn't love you and pined for another woman? For what? So I could inherit the keys to the kingdom?" He chuckled wryly. "Well, you can see what good that did you. He screwed you over yet again."

"He screwed us both, Max," his mother responded tightly. "He's given half your birthright over to that no-good playboy brother of yours."

Maximus eyed her warily. "Be careful, Mother. Be very careful."

"Why? Don't tell me you're feeling sentimental about a brother you never knew you had and who's trying to take what's rightfully yours."

Maximus didn't believe for a second that was the case. Lucius had been as shocked as he was by the bequest. He hadn't known he was Arthur's son until that moment in the hospital a couple of weeks ago, when his mother had railed at him. Maximus had seen the horror that had crossed his older brother's face when the realization had sunk in that not only had his mother been carrying on an affair for decades with their father, but that he'd been the result of it. Lucius had been devastated.

Despite that, however, Maximus wasn't about to let an interloper, an outsider, walk in and take what was his. He'd been groomed his entire life to run Knight Shipping, and *no one*, brother or no brother, or their sexy partner, Tahlia Armstrong, would get in his way. He would see to it.

"Of course I'm not sentimental, Mother," Maximus responded. "But haven't you heard the old phrase 'you catch more flies with honey'? Don't worry."

Her brown eyes stared at him incredulously. "How can I not be worried when half your inheritance is being stolen?"

"We have to play it cool, Mother. Because if there's one thing I've learned in business, it's that we mustn't show our hand. I promise you, I'll get what's mine. I promise you. All in due time."

"How?"

"I have a plan."

Chapter 2

"You own Art Gallery Twenty-One?" Kaitlynn Armstrong, Tahlia's sister, stared back openmouthed as they sat at Tahlia's breakfast bar the next morning. Tahlia had stopped by Kaitlynn's apartment to tell her about the dinner at the Knights' estate and to share her amazing news and good fortune.

"Sure do," Tahlia replied with a self-satisfied smile. "Arthur Knight transferred the title to me. So now that witch Bailey will be coming to me for approval."

Tahlia was referring to her boss, Bailey Smith, who was into traditional art. Tahlia had been trying unsuccessfully to get her to branch out to show unconventional pieces. It was only when Arthur had liked a piece from an up-and-coming artist that Bailey had relented for a small showing. It was at that opening that Tahlia had first laid eyes on Maximus Knight.

She'd been setting out canapés when he'd walked into Art Gallery Twenty-One just as confident as he pleased in a designer suit, skinny tie and expensive loafers. He looked every bit the wealthy shipping magnate. From her vantage point, he'd looked serious and intent when he'd spoken to his father. Tahlia had watched him from afar, soaking in every bit of his aura, from the curly fro on his head that she would love to run her fingers through to the bushy eyebrows above sexy eyes to those sinful lips.

Unfortunately, Maximus Knight hadn't stayed long at the gallery. She'd been pulled away to help a customer, and when she'd finally looked for him, he'd been gone. But now everything had changed. Arthur's death had set her on a new path that Tahlia could only hope she could prove worthy of.

"I still can't believe it," Kaitlynn said. "Did you have any idea that Arthur Knight put you in his will?"

Tahlia shook her head. "None."

"Have you told Mom yet?"

"No, not yet. She's at work now," Tahlia responded. Their mother, Sophia, was an RN at UCLA Medical Center and had just started her evening shift. And Tahlia couldn't possibly tell her this news over the phone. *This news* had to be delivered in person.

Kaitlynn glanced down at her Apple watch. "Oh, yeah, right. I'd forgotten. She'll just die when she hears the news."

"Just like I did," Tahlia responded. "It's so surreal."

"Why do you think Arthur did it?"

Tahlia shrugged. "All I can think of is that I was kind to him. Sometimes he'd come in on his lunch break to just stare at the paintings. He'd be so wistful that I'd come over and chat with him. I could tell something weighed on his mind heavily at times, but he never shared with me the full details."

"So you had no idea he was carrying on an affair?"

"Of course not. But I did know he had another son whom he had treated unfairly. I suspect Arthur regretted his actions, which is why he's taken such drastic actions now in his will."

"But to make *you* the deciding vote?" Kaitlynn said. "That's heady stuff. He clearly thought very highly of you, sis."

"I feel honored," Tahlia said, lightly touching her chest. "And scared out of my wits. I mean, Kaitlynn, I know nothing about the shipping business."

"Perhaps Maximus will teach you." She grinned with a wink. "I think you'd like that, wouldn't you?"

Tahlia jumped up from her stool to cover the blush she could feel creeping up her cheeks. "Why would you say that?"

"C'mon," Kaitlynn teased. "I've seen how you react whenever Maximus is mentioned in the news or on social media. You've got a crush on him," she said in a singsongy tone.

"Do not," Tahlia said, spinning around to face her.

"Preach to the choir because I'm not listening." She covered her ears with her hands.

"Even if I did," Tahlia responded with her hands on her hips, "I doubt Maximus would be interested in a peon like me."

"I beg to differ. You're in a position of power now, and Maximus will have no choice but to stand up and take notice of you."

"Because of the shares I have?"

"You're the deciding vote," Kaitlynn responded. "He'll want to keep you close. The question is how close will you let him get?"

Tahlia smiled at Kaitlynn's teasing tone. She'd wanted Maximus to see her, but she would rather it was because he genuinely found her interesting, not because he thought she was a pawn he could use. But perhaps if they spent some time together he'd see her as something more than a vote in his favor. Only time would tell just what her relationship with Maximus would be.

"This is stunning news, Max," his best friend, Griffin Cooper, stated when they met up on Sunday at the Los Angeles Country Club. Now seated in the main dining room, they were sharing breakfast over a cup of coffee. They'd forgone their weekly racquetball session to just sit and talk.

"You're telling me," Maximus replied. "I knew my father was a cunning liar, but I never in my wildest dreams imagined he would cut me out of what's rightfully mine."

"You've worked your butt off for Knight Shipping," Griffin concurred. "It's not fair."

"No, it isn't." Maximus seethed in his seat. He'd been awake for nearly half the night mulling the situation over, remembering everything he'd ever done to win his father's favor. The countless times he'd made sure to excel in school, to be the best in sports, to get into Harvard Business School, and still it was never quite enough. His father always pushed and pushed him. And for what? So in the end he could share running Knight Shipping with Lucius? And Tahlia Armstrong? Where in the heck had she come from?

"Why do you think he did it?"

"At first, I was so sucker punched, I couldn't think of a single reason why. And then it came to me."

"What came to you? Don't leave me in suspense."

"Tahlia may think my father's motives were altruistic in giving her those shares. And maybe they were." Maximus's lips twisted in a cynical smile. "But I suspect the old man wanted to ensure that I never took Knight Shipping public."

Griffin's expression grew still, and he became serious. "Do you really think he went that far?"

Maximus shrugged.

"What are you going to do?" Griffin inquired. "Contest it? I would imagine your father made the will ironclad." Griffin was an attorney at a well-known law firm in Los Angeles.

Maximus nodded. "Robert said as much."

"So? Do you think Lucius will sign over his shares?"

"It's doubtful," Maximus responded. Despite the fact that Lucius hadn't asked for or even wanted the inheritance, Maximus doubted he'd walk away from it. His older brother struck him as the proud type. He'd keep the shares, just to show Maximus that he could and to prove to himself that he could run it. He'd done his research, and Lucius hadn't become a corporate raider by chance. Lucius had obtained an MBA before investing in his first business venture, an up-and-coming technology firm. The gamble paid off, and he'd made his first million before he was thirty.

Unlike Maximus, who'd been groomed since he was young that one day he'd take over the company Arthur had started with his mother Charlotte's help. Oh, yes, Maximus had learned years ago that his father had married into money and had used her family's money to start Knight Shipping. No doubt, that was why he'd stayed married to her because he didn't want to lose his empire. Yet, he continued his affair with Jocelyn Turner, the woman he'd truly loved.

It burned in Maximus's craw.

"Max?" Griffin interrupted his thoughts. "What are you thinking? I can see your mind spinning a mile a minute. Are you thinking about the overseas deal and how you're going to salvage it?"

Knight Shipping had been offered lucrative contracts to transport electrical machinery and luxury vehicles, but they needed capital to expand, especially if Knight Shipping wanted to compete with the other cargo and shipping companies in the Port of Los Angeles marketplace.

"I am thinking about it. But there's no getting around Lucius," Maximus responded, "at least for the moment. I'll have to choose a different route."

Griffin studied him, trying to read his next move. "The girl?"

"Bingo." Maximus smiled devilishly.

"How?"

"Get her on my side. Convince her to see things my way."

"And how do you plan to do that?" Griffin inquired, sipping his coffee.

Maximus shrugged. "It's quite easy. Seduce her."

Griffin choked on his beverage. "Excuse me?"

"You heard me. Tahlia Armstrong likes me," Maximus replied. "I sensed it yesterday when she stayed behind for dinner."

"Your mother dined with the woman who'd been carrying on an affair with her husband for years?" Griffin was aghast.

"Trust me, it didn't last long. But it was Tahlia's idea. From what I gather, my father intended her to be the peacekeeper between Lucius and me. Last night was her first attempt, which although a bust gave me just the ammunition I need to get out of this quagmire my father has left us in. I mean really, Griff, he gave both of us forty-nine percent? What was he thinking?"

"He wasn't. He felt guilty for keeping Lucius in the dark about his true identity. This was his way of making amends."

"At my expense," Max said hotly. "He could have given Lucius money, baubles, anything—even a smaller percentage of the company. Why did he have to give him an equal share in Knight Shipping? He knew how much the company meant to me. The only thing I can think of is he did this to spite me, get back at me in some way because I was never the son he really wanted."

Griffin frowned. "What do you mean?"

"Isn't it obvious? He wanted Jocelyn. He wanted their son, Lucius, but he could never have them because he was bound to my mother because her money was used to build his company."

"C'mon, Maximus. That sounds twisted. I'm sure that's not it."

"Isn't it?" Maximus had never truly felt loved by his father. Arthur had been happy to see him go away to boarding school and college. And when he'd come home, Maximus would be so happy to see him and eager to show his father the reports of how well he'd done, but Arthur could never be bothered. He was always working. For what? A company he told Max would be his, only to give half of it away to Lucius, the son he really wanted?

"Max, bro." Griffin grabbed his shoulder from across the table. "Don't. Don't do this to yourself. Don't second-guess everything that ever happened between you and your father. It'll drive you crazy."

"No crazier than learning my entire life was built on a lie," Maximus stated harshly, shrugging Griffin's hand away. "Finding out my father married my mother for her money and only stayed with her because of it.

He never loved her *or* me. We were both just a means to an end."

"Max…"

Maximus rose to his feet and buttoned his suit jacket. "Anyway, thanks for hearing out me, Griff. I guess I just needed to get some things off my chest."

Griffin stood, as well. "Of course. Anytime you need an ear, I'm here to listen."

Maximus turned to leave, but Griffin stopped him.

"What about Tahlia Armstrong? Were you serious about your intentions toward her?"

Maximus hesitated in his footsteps. No, he wasn't sure this was the right move. He didn't relish hurting anyone, least of all an unsuspecting, sweet and beautiful woman like Tahlia Armstrong, but his hands were tied. "It's the only way."

Tahlia stood outside Art Gallery Twenty-One in the Arts District on Monday morning and looked up at the white stucco two-story building. She still couldn't believe she *owned* it, lock, stock and barrel. Arthur Knight had purchased the art gallery on her behalf and bequeathed it to her in his will.

A smile formed on Tahlia's full lips. He'd done this for her. When all she'd ever done was listen to the older gentleman when he came to look at artwork. She'd had no idea that small act of kindness would lend itself to Arthur being so generous.

"How long are you going to stand outside?" asked Faith Richardson, a petite blonde with a luscious mane of hair that Tahlia would kill for. Faith was one of the main reasons she'd stayed at the gallery. In addition to sharing a love of art, they were also friends as well as coworkers. Of course, she wouldn't be a coworker for too much longer once Tahlia shared her news.

Tahlia couldn't wait for the opportunity to tell Bailey Smith who was boss now.

"Oh, I'm coming in," Tahlia said as Faith swung open the double glass doors into the gallery.

Every time she did, Tahlia loved how wide, open and airy the gallery was. With its white walls, covered with paintings and other works of art, it was her dream come true to exhibit at a place like this. She'd never imagined that one day she'd own it.

"There you are," Bailey Smith, Tahlia's boss, stated as they arrived. "You're late."

The slender brunette was wearing a scowl as Tahlia and Faith approached her, though Tahlia had to admit she was looking ever the fashionista in a navy pantsuit and cream silk top and was no doubt wearing designer heels. Meanwhile, Tahlia was her usual self in a twisted-drape pencil skirt and an off-the-shoulder sweater with a slew of dangling necklaces.

Bailey flashed a disapproving look at her ensemble before starting in on her. "How many times must I remind you about promptness, Tahlia?"

Tahlia sighed. "I've lost count." It was only a few minutes after 9:00 a.m., and there were no patrons in the gallery. Most didn't arrive until just before noon. She didn't understand why Bailey insisted on riding her. It wasn't like she didn't stay late when needed.

"Then I would think you'd remember to be on time," Bailey reminded, "but that's inconsequential. I've just been told that our new owner will be arriving to this morning's staff meeting. Come, the attorney is here."

She ushered them toward the back of the house where

Bailey's office, Tahlia and Faith's even smaller office and the small kitchenette were housed.

When she arrived, Tahlia found Robert Kellogg, Arthur's attorney, already seated. She smiled and he returned it with one of his own. Only the two of them knew what she was privy to but would soon be revealed to the group.

Tahlia took a seat at the six-seater table while Bailey sat at the head of the table with Robert and Faith flanking her to her left.

"Mr. Kellogg, we're very eager to hear news of the new owner," Bailey began. "Please fill us in."

"And I am eager to share with you," Robert returned.

"I'm just so sorry to hear of Mr. Knight's passing. He was a lover of the arts. Of course, I had no idea he actually owned the gallery." Bailey chuckled nervously.

"He preferred to keep his interests private," Robert said, looking in Tahlia's direction.

Bailey glanced at Tahlia with a raised brow. Could she tell that the gauntlet was about to drop on her? Tahlia was just happy that Robert was here to give the news.

"As I mentioned to you a couple of days ago, Ms. Smith," Robert began, "the reading of Arthur Knight's will occurred yesterday and Arthur Knight was named as owner of Art Gallery Twenty-One, and he bequeathed it...."

"Will his son Maximus be taking over the gallery?" Bailey asked, interrupting him.

"No, Arthur had someone else in mind."

Bailey's eyes lit up with anticipation. "Who, then?"

Robert turned to face Tahlia. "Ms. Smith, meet the new owner of Art Gallery Twenty-One."

"W-what?" Bailey's eyes grew wide with disbelief. "I—I don't understand."

"Omigod!" Faith's hand flew to her mouth.

"All right, then let me be clear. Arthur Knight bequeathed the gallery to Ms. Armstrong. She is the gallery's new owner." He slid the deed of ownership over to Tahlia.

"That simply can't be," Bailey said. "Why would he do such a thing? She—" Bailey motioned toward Tahlia "—is a lowly gallery assistant, while I have been running this gallery for over three years."

Robert shrugged and closed his briefcase. "I don't know what to tell you, but the will is a fait accompli. Ms. Armstrong." He glanced at Tahlia, who couldn't resist sporting a huge grin at Bailey's disbelief that *she* actually owned the gallery. "If you need anything, please—" he handed her his business card "—give me a call. Arthur asked me to be at your disposal for whatever questions you might have as you take on your new ventures."

"Ventures? As in plural?" Bailey inquired incredulously. "What else did he give you?"

"Good day." Robert nodded at Tahlia and left the room, leaving the three women sitting at the table.

"This is such great news," Faith said and rushed from around the table to give Tahlia a warm hug. "I can't believe it. You own the gallery. But why don't you seem surprised? Did you know already?"

Tahlia nodded. "I received a letter from Mr. Kellogg that Arthur requested the gallery be given to me upon his death, but I didn't have the actual paperwork until now." She held up the deed in her hand.

"You!" The one word from Bailey that came across

the table was bitter and caused Tahlia and Faith to both look up in alarm.

Bailey's normally porcelain skin was red with fury. "You own the gallery! What did you do? Sleep with the old man?" She laughed. "You must have. How else to explain why a wealthy man like Arthur Knight would give a gallery to you, a peon, a nobody."

Anger boiled in Tahlia's veins. She wouldn't be put down by this woman a second longer. She'd been Bailey's whipping boy—or girl, for that matter—for two years, but no more. "Watch yourself, Bailey. Be very, very careful before you utter another word."

"Why? Because you'll fire me?" Bailey laughed, throwing her head back. "Well, don't bother. I quit!"

"Good, you've made my life easy," Tahlia responded, facing the angry-faced woman. "I don't have to fire you. Please pack your belongings and don't let the door hit you on the way out."

Bailey took a step toward Tahlia. "You've no idea how to run this gallery. Mark my words, you'll be out of business within the year because you're a flighty ditz."

"Get out!"

"Gladly." Bailey stormed from the conference room.

Tahlia followed Bailey to her office. She watched her open and close drawers and bang items around as she packed a box. She was keeping an eye on the woman because she wouldn't put it past Bailey to try to sabotage her. Her former boss was packed in five minutes flat and stalking toward the front door, her stilettos hitting the wood floor like spikes. When the door finally slammed behind her, Tahlia let out a long sigh of relief and leaned against one of the walls.

"Wow! That was dramatic," Faith commented from behind her.

Tahlia breathed in deeply before she spoke. "Yes, it was. I just hope she wasn't right."

"Right about what?" Faith asked, folding her arms across her chest. "About you failing? That's a lot of hogwash. Bailey just had sour grapes because Arthur Knight didn't leave her the gallery. Though I shouldn't be surprised it was you. You and he always did have a special bond."

"Yeah, we did." Tahlia became wistful as she glanced at one of the benches where they used to sit. With her father gone, Arthur had been like a father figure to her, filling a void she hadn't known she'd needed filled until she had someone to confide in about her hopes, her dreams and her fears. She remembered sitting with Arthur during his lunch hour and talking at length. He hadn't wanted to go back to the office. Instead, he wished he was in the Louvre in Paris. With Lucius's mother, perhaps?

"Don't worry." Faith reached across and patted Tahlia's arm. "You'll do great. You've always had tons of great ideas that Bailey would never listen to. But this place—" she spread her arms wide "—is yours now. And you can do with it as you please. Invite whatever artists you want to exhibit."

Tahlia beamed as she stood up from the wall. "You're right. We're—" she pointed to Faith "—going to do great things here. And Bailey Smith will rue the day she ever underestimated me."

And so would Maximus Xavier Knight. If Kaitlynn was right in her assumption that he would try to charm her, then Tahlia was going to have to have her wits about her.

Chapter 3

Maximus pulled his blue Bugatti sports car in front of Art Gallery Twenty-One later that evening. He'd tried unsuccessfully to make it earlier so he could invite Tahlia out for lunch. His schedule had been an endless array of meetings as he tried to keep Knight Shipping clients calm. They were all worried with Arthur's death about the status of the company. And quite frankly, so was Maximus. How was he supposed to run a company with only half the power? He needed to be free and clear to make decisions unilaterally. But those days were gone. He'd have to consult big brother Lucius as well as Tahlia on every major decision that he made. The machinery deal had stalled, but the luxury vehicle opportunity was still on the horizon. They had to strike while the iron was hot.

Damn his father for putting him in this position!

He'd always done everything that was asked of him and more. And this was how he was repaid, with a knife in the back? Or at least that was how it felt to Maximus. While Lucius and Tahlia were laughing all the way to the bank. Speaking of Tahlia…

Maximus glanced at the whitewashed stucco building. Inside was the woman who held the key to whether his running of Knight Shipping would go smoothly or whether it would be hell on earth. He needed Tahlia on his side. He could offer to buy her shares outright, but if she said no then that would cloud anything that transpired between them after that. No, better to wait. Maximus hoped that with a little schmoozing Tahlia would vote to effectively neutralize Lucius. Just how far he would go to make that happen remained to be seen.

He'd told Griffin he intended to seduce Tahlia, but Maximus was hoping it wouldn't come to that. Maybe Tahlia would see things his way and need very little convincing. Exiting his vehicle, he strode purposefully toward the door.

The gallery was well lit with vibrant paintings adorning the walls and several sculptures strategically placed throughout the open floor plan on pedestals or suspended from the ceiling. It was nearly closing time, so there were less than a handful of people milling about the room. Maximus strolled through the gallery, peering at several pieces of artwork. He'd come once before for an artist's exhibition, but he'd hardly seen any of it. He'd come here that night to talk to his father because he'd left the office early before they'd closed a deal. He'd found Arthur hadn't been interested in discussing business. So Maximus had stayed on his phone until the deal was finalized. But now he had time to look around to see what his father had seen in this place.

He stopped in front of a particularly intriguing painting.

"It's quite complex, yes?" a soft feminine voice said from his side.

Maximus glanced sideways and saw that Tahlia had joined him and was looking at the painting. "Yes, it is."

"I've told the artist that he should dig deeper like he did with this piece. I think he's very talented."

"Is there more of his work here?"

Tahlia shook her head. "At the time, I could only convince my boss to exhibit one."

"Shouldn't be a problem for you now," Maximus stated, moving from the painting to walk toward another, "now that you own the gallery." He noticed that Tahlia followed behind him.

"No, it won't be," she responded, "but why does that sound like an accusation?"

He turned to face her and offered an apologetic smile. "I'm sorry. I didn't intend it that way. I was merely stating the obvious, which is you're a wealthy woman now and the gallery is yours to run as you see fit."

She eyed him suspiciously, as if she didn't believe him. "Yes, it does, and I have some ideas."

"Care to share them over dinner?" Maximus inquired. He glanced down at his watch. "It's about closing time, isn't it?"

"Yes, it is, but I would need a few minutes to shut down."

"That's no problem," he responded. "I can wait."

"Why would you?"

"I thought it might be a good idea to get to know my business partner since we'll be working together."

She nodded. "Yes, I suppose that makes sense."

"Then join me." He trained his dark brown eyes on hers.

"All right," she replied. "Give me a few minutes, okay?"

"Sure thing. I'll just mosey around."

He stared at her retreating figure. He shouldn't want Tahlia, but he did on some elemental, visceral level. Every time he looked into her eyes, they sizzled with fire, blasting through every reserve in his arsenal. He had not felt anything with his previous lovers other than the physical release his body craved, but there was something about Tahlia that triggered an untapped need in him to care for her, guard her. He had to figure out what it was. He couldn't afford any distractions, not if he wanted to keep what was his.

From the loft above, Tahlia stared down at Maximus as he moved through the gallery like a sleek panther hunting his next game. And was that her? Was that why he was here?

He'd said it was because they were going to be partners at Knight Shipping, but Tahlia didn't believe him—at least not entirely. The way he'd looked at her told her it might be something more personal. She wouldn't mind if it were. Maximus Knight was a gorgeous man. And tonight she'd been made increasingly aware of that fact.

She'd been stunned when after finishing up with a customer, she'd noticed him in *her* gallery staring at one of her favorite paintings. Since he hadn't noticed her, she'd been able to soak him in. Power radiated from the man—along with a killer instinct, which she was sure served him well in the business world. But there was a sophistication and polish to Maximus that came from being born into money. And his looks—he was well-groomed with a boldly handsome face that appealed to her. The tiny curling tendrils encircling his head made Tahlia want to reach out and finger them. He stood proud and strong in an arresting dark suit that outlined his shoulders and towering presence.

He was, however, deep in thought, and she'd wondered what could have him so perplexed. And so she'd stepped toward him, eager to find out. His compelling gaze made Tahlia nearly lose her breath, but she'd put up a good front. She knew he wasn't happy about her new role in his company.

If she'd had her pick, it wasn't the role Tahlia would have chosen, either. She'd have wanted Maximus to notice *her* because he'd found her attractive. And maybe he did, but she suspected he was spending time with her now only to try to figure out where she stood. And exactly where was that?

Tahlia wasn't sure, but maybe she'd figure it out tonight.

Maximus watched Tahlia saunter toward him. His eyes roved over her figure, and he missed nothing. Not the way the drape of the skirt hugged her curves or how the sleek sweater showed off her naked shoulders. His tongue flicked out to moisten his parched lips. Tahlia was mighty fine. And Maximus had to admit, he would enjoy his dinner companion for the evening.

"Ready to go?" he asked when she made it to him. Her large expressive eyes were alive and glowing, and Maximus liked what he saw there. She was most certainly interested in him, which could play into his game if he decided to go there.

"Yes, let's do it." She headed through the doors. He stayed close behind her as she locked up, so when she turned around her face was mere inches from his.

"Oh." She stepped back for a moment and nearly

stumbled, so Maximus reached out and circled his arm around her waist.

"Careful."

They stayed that way for several seconds, both of them staring at each other. Maximus looked her over seductively, and when his gaze went to her full lips, he felt her tense almost immediately and she stepped away.

"Where to?" she asked, moving toward the sidewalk. "I'll follow behind you."

"We should take my car," Maximus said. "I don't mind driving."

"That isn't necessary."

"I insist."

In the end, Maximus won out and he opened the passenger door for Tahlia to his Bugatti, and she slid inside. He came around to the driver's side, hopped in and started the engine. Tahlia seemed uneasy beside him as he drove to dinner despite the fact that she looked damn good in the red leather bucket seat. After several long, excruciating silent minutes, Maximus patted her thigh. "Relax, Tahlia. I don't bite."

"Are you sure about that?"

He grinned. "What have you heard? Or should I say read?"

"You have a reputation for being determined."

It seemed like she'd thought that word through very carefully. "You mean ruthless?"

"That word has been used."

"And you're wondering how it applies to you?"

"Shouldn't I?" Tahlia asked. "I know I stand in the way of something you want."

"Who's to say you're not what I want?" Maximus said as he pulled into the valet area of a well-known French bistro. He glanced at Tahlia and saw the stunned look on her face, just as he exited the vehicle and handed his keys to the valet.

He was at her door in no time, grasping her hand and pulling her from the vehicle. He liked touching her and that when he did, her reaction to him was purely physically. He planned to keep on touching her. With his hand at the small of her back, he led her inside the bistro.

"Jean George," Maximus greeted the maître d'.

"Mr. Knight," Jean George replied. "It's a pleasure to have you dining with us again. Your same table, I presume?"

"If it's available."

"For you, of course. Please allow me." He led Tahlia and Maximus to a quiet booth away from the bustling interior.

Tahlia slid inside the booth, and Maximus eased in beside her. When their thighs began to touch, Maximus felt his skin prickle and heat up in awareness. Or was it the playful scent of her peony fragrance that permeated the small space they shared? They both peered at their menus for several moments, but Maximus didn't need to look; he knew what he wanted.

When Tahlia glanced up, she found his gaze was riveted on her. "What are you doing, Maximus?"

"Call me Max. All my friends do."

"And is that what we are, friends?"

"We don't have to be enemies," he stated firmly.

"I guess that depends on you," Tahlia stated, and his eyebrow rose. Tahlia wasn't as naive as he imagined her to be.

A waiter came over and took their drink orders, a scotch for Maximus and a club soda for Tahlia. Once he'd gone, Maximus responded to Tahlia's comment.

"All right, I'll bite. I didn't anticipate having you or Lucius to answer to when running my company."

"Don't you mean *our company*?" she responded quickly.

He was about to correct her when he saw the smile in her eyes. She was teasing him. "All my life I've been groomed to run Knight Shipping, so imagine how you would feel if the shoe was on the other foot and interlopers came in to tell you how to run it."

"I can only imagine that you feel slighted, as would I," Tahlia said. "But this doesn't have to be a battle between you and your brother, Lucius."

"And how do you foresee this going, Tahlia?"

He liked how her name rolled off his lips.

Tahlia shrugged. "I'm not sure. We'll have to make it up as we go along."

At her words, he frowned. Maximus didn't leave anything to chance. He was all about facts and figures and making a well-thought-out educated decision before proceeding in life as well as in business. It was why he'd been so successful.

"Listen, no one said this was going to be easy. I think your father put me in the middle to help negotiate a peaceful truce between the two of you."

"You don't resent that he's put you in the middle of an untenable position?"

"At first, I did," she answered honestly, "but then I began to see it as an honor and that I could make a difference."

"Are you always this positive?" Maximus inquired, steepling his fingers and staring at her. "Because that's sort of a Pollyanna way of thinking."

"That might be so, but I'm here and I'm not going away."

There was never a truer statement, Maximus thought. "No, you're not, so we might as well get to know each other if we're going to be spending so much time together."

"At the office, I presume."

The waiter returned and set both their drinks on the table.

After they'd ordered dinner, Maximus immediately reached for his drink and took a sip. "As a shareholder in Knight shipping, your presence, although not required, is expected at functions in town or around the globe if needed."

"I only own two percent. You and Lucius have the lion's share. You don't need me there." Tahlia reached for her beverage and drank liberally from her club soda.

"What if I want you there?" Maximus countered.

Tahlia looked up at him through thick lashes, and Maximus's stomach lurched. He did want her around and not just for business. He wanted her for himself. He wanted to get to know her story and how she'd become this beacon of positivity.

"I—I'll be there, if I'm needed."

She didn't rise to his bait, but that was okay. Maximus wasn't sure where this was going, but there was an attraction between them. He felt it because his heartbeat was thumping at a rapid pace and he couldn't take his eyes off her and vice versa. She was looking at him like she wanted to jump his bones. And if she did, Maximus wouldn't mind at all.

"So, Tahlia, tell me your story." He drank a bit more of his scotch and regarded her with interest.

"You mean you haven't researched the interloper who just burst into your life?"

He stared at her long and hard until she looked downward. "No, I haven't. I was hoping to do that *person-ally*."

"All right," she said. "What do you want to know?"

"Everything."

"That's very vague. Hmm…" She paused. "I guess I can tell you that I was raised by my mother, Sophia Armstrong. It's always been Mama, Kaitlynn—that's my baby sister—and me. My mother is an RN at UCLA Medical Center, and my sister is an accountant."

"And your father? You didn't mention him. Where's he in the picture?"

"He was mugged and shot one night coming home from work. He—he didn't survive his injuries."

Maximus noted how formal she sounded about losing her father so young. It had to have been devastating for her. "How old were you?"

"Ten years old," Tahlia said. "Kaitlynn was only six. She barely remembers him, but I do. He was such a good dad. He taught me how to ride a bike, he helped me with my homework. He tucked me into bed at night and read us stories…" Her voice trailed off, and he could see the toll talking about it was having on her. Her eyes had become misty and wet with tears.

Maximus reached across the table, placed his hand over hers and squeezed. She didn't move away. Instead, she let him comfort her, and he used his other hand to wipe away an errant tear that slid down her cheek. When she looked up at him, so soft and tender, all Maximus wanted was to wrap her in his arms and kiss her until the hurt went way. Instead, he just slid closer and wrapped his arm around her, and they sat silently for several minutes.

"I'm sorry," he finally said.

"No, I'm sorry. I didn't mean to get emotional. I

just get choked up talking about my dad sometimes."
Tahlia sniffed.

Maximus turned to her, offering her his handkerchief. "Don't be, you loved him. And it shows. I don't think I've even cried over my father since his death."

She glanced up at him through lashes damp with tears as she dabbed at her eyes with the hanky. "You haven't?"

"We didn't have the sort of relationship that you and your father did." He finished off the rest of his scotch and placed the empty glass on the table.

"You didn't?" She sounded incredulous as she moved out of his embrace to look inquiringly at him.

"That surprises you?"

"If I'm honest?" she asked. "It does. Arthur was always so caring toward me. And I suppose losing my dad so young that having Arthur in my life was a godsend. We had a special relationship that went beyond a love of art, but was genuine."

"Then I envy you," Maximus said. "Because my father was never affectionate with me. In fact, it was quite the opposite. Whenever I seemed to be around, he was cold, distant and indifferent. Which is why I'm still boggled over why he stayed with my mother. And the only thing I've come up with is money. He stayed with her for money and the power that came with it.

"No." Tahlia shook her head. "That can't be. I can't reconcile that with the Arthur I knew."

"Then you didn't know him at all. He was a master of lies."

"But he loved you. He loved both his sons."

"He did?" Now it was Maximus's turn to be in disbelief. He'd shared so much with a stranger, but yet he hadn't been able to tell his own sons those words? It didn't make any sense. He was understanding Arthur Knight less and less with each passing day.

At the stunned look on Maximus's face, Tahlia knew she'd said the wrong thing. She'd thought her words would give him comfort, but they were having the opposite effect. "I'm so sorry, Maximus. I don't know why Arthur wasn't honest with both his sons about his true feelings. I only know he wanted to claim his other son. But he never revealed it was Lucius. Just that it was his wish that both of you would run the business together one day."

Maximus snorted. "For an outsider, you sure do know a lot about my family. Or should I say my father? It appears as if maybe you did know him better than any of us." He signaled the waiter over.

"I'll have another scotch." He turned to Tahlia. "What would you like?"

"Nothing for me."

The waiter departed, leaving them alone again. Tahlia noticed Maximus was silent as he pondered her words. Arthur Knight was a mix of contradictions. He was outwardly cold to Maximus and his mother, Charlotte, passionate with Jocelyn Turner and a father figure to her. And now Maximus would never know the answer to the burning questions he must have.

"Max," Tahlia began. "What can I do?"

He frowned. "I'm not sure you can do anything, Tahlia. You're in the middle of this mess, and we'll have to navigate our way through it."

Tahlia didn't like his answer, and she wished she'd never told him just how much Arthur had shared with her. She hadn't meant to hurt Maximus, but it was clear she had. His father had been open with her and not him. That had to sting.

She tried to change the subject. "I never got to finish my story," she said. "You asked me about myself."

"Hmm… I did, didn't I?" Maximus sipped his scotch. "Why don't you tell me how you got involved with the gallery?"

His question brought a smile to Tahlia's face. "Actually, I'm an artist."

He peered at her with intensity. "You are? Then why are you *working* at the gallery and not exhibiting?"

Tahlia shrugged. "I wasn't very successful at getting my own art displayed, so I thought what better way to stay in the field than to help other struggling artists?"

"And your own art? What became of it?"

"I still dabble."

"Would you show me your work sometime?" he inquired.

A smile of enchantment crossed Tahlia's lips at the request. "Yes, I would like that."

"It's a date," Maximus said. His look was so galvanizing it sent a tremor through Tahlia, and her heart began hammering loudly in her ears. She wanted to respond and tell him she'd love to go out with him again, but a knot rose in her throat and all Tahlia could do was nod.

The waiter brought their entrées and they both dug into their French meals. The food was rich and decadent, but delicious. Tahlia had no qualms about finishing the meal, and Maximus commented on it.

"You enjoyed your meal?" He inclined his head to her empty plate.

She blushed. "I'd think that was obvious." She wiped the corners of her mouth with a napkin.

"I love this place and come here often," Maximus said. "It might be small and quaint, but I believe in quality over quantity, and the food is best—thus why I have a special table."

"Thank you for the invite."

"You're welcome. Would you care for dessert? Coffee?"

She patted her stomach. "Oh, no, I couldn't eat another thing."

"All right, I'll get the bill." He motioned the waiter over.

Once the bill was settled, Maximus and Tahlia made their way back to the valet station. And once his Bugatti was procured, they were on their way back to the gallery, where Tahlia's car was parked. Conversation continued until they arrived at the deserted parking lot. Maximus pulled up alongside her VW Bug. Next to his Bugatti, her car looked like a relic, but because she'd been a struggling artist, it was all she could afford at the time. Though now, she could afford much more. But Tahlia was determined not to be frivolous. Robert had offered to help her, and she suspected she'd need all the help she could get, starting with an accountant and a financial adviser.

"I enjoyed tonight," Tahlia said, once Maximus had opened the passenger door and walked her to her car. She stood at the door ready to glide in, but something in the way he was looking at her held Tahlia back.

Was he going to kiss her?

If he were, she wouldn't stop him. She'd welcome it after the wonderful night she'd spent in his company. Last year, when she'd seen him from across the room looking so deliciously handsome, she'd secretly wondered what it would be like to *be* with Maximus, but for now she'd settle for a kiss.

"So did I. And I'd like to see you again." He leaned forward toward her, pressing Tahlia backward into the driver's door. "Perhaps you can come to Knight Shipping? I could give you a tour of the facilities. You can see for yourself what you've inherited."

"You'd do that?" Tahlia asked softly, looking at his sinful lips. She ached for them to brush hers.

"For you, yes." His mouth was so very near hers.

"But not for Lucius?" she inquired. The ire on Maximus's face at the mention of his older brother's name had Tahlia immediately regretting her choice to bring him into the conversation.

Maximus straightened and took a step backward. "I extended the invitation to you, but I suppose I might as well get it over with, so fine, invite him. Have a good night, Tahlia."

He turned on his heel to leave, which meant he wasn't going to kiss her tonight. She'd put her foot in her mouth because of her do-gooder ways.

"I will," Tahlia said to his retreating figure as she watched him get into his sports car and drive off. She clicked opened her car and slid in. Then she slammed her fists on the steering wheel. Why hadn't she kept her mouth shut? Her hands flew up to her lips. If she had, she was certain Maximus would have kissed her, and now she wouldn't know the feel of his mouth on hers. Would she ever?

As he drove away, Maximus realized he had Tahlia exactly where he wanted her. Or did he? Tonight hadn't gone exactly as he anticipated it would. The impending deals that would lead to expansion and going public had been far from his mind. Instead, his purpose had been to find out more about Tahlia, and he had. She'd grown up fatherless, a struggling artist needing someone to look after her. There was a certain naïveté and innocence about her that intrigued Maximus and apparently his father, too.

Arthur Knight had been the father Tahlia no longer had, but then their relationship had changed and she'd become his confidante. He'd shared secrets with Tahlia about his wishes that he could never share with his own family until his death. But she didn't appear to be using that knowledge with malice or avarice. Or at least none that Maximus could see. She also seemed steadfast in her intent to ensure that he and Lucius formed a brotherhood, as if that were possible.

It wasn't.

Maximus may not fault Lucius for his existence, but he didn't share. Knight Shipping was his and his alone because he'd earned it. Lucius and Tahlia stood in the way of that. Maximus had to neutralize Lucius's power. The only way to do that was to get to Tahlia. And tonight he had.

She'd wanted him to kiss her as much as he'd wanted to. And he might have, if she'd had the good sense to leave Lucius out of the conversation. Instead, she would have to wait, wait until Maximus decided it was time. He didn't relish seducing Tahlia and the potential of ruining the positive bubble she lived in, but there was no way around it.

He would have to be smart about it, though. Slowly court Tahlia until she didn't notice that he had her under his thumb. But at the same time Maximus would have to keep his heart locked up tight because something told him if he wasn't careful, he'd fall under Tahlia's spell.

Chapter 4

"You own this place?" Tahlia's mother, Sophia, said when she and Kaitlynn returned from taking Tahlia out for lunch several days later. It was her mother's day off from the hospital, and she'd finally had the time to come by and see Tahlia's new venture.

"I do," Tahlia said with a wide grin. She'd already made some small changes by rearranging the artwork throughout the rooms and reaching out to several artists she'd recommended to Bailey, who'd dismissed them without ever reviewing their work. Tahlia was looking forward to showcasing their talent at a future exhibition.

"Will you show your own work, too?" Kaitlynn asked, turning around to face her sister.

"Max asked me the same thing."

"Max?" Kaitlynn's brow furrowed at her use of his nickname.

"Maximus," Tahlia repeated.

"As in Maximus Knight of Knight Shipping?" her mother stated. Apparently, even her mother had heard of him.

Tahlia nodded. "Yes, that's the other part of the surprise I have in store for you."

Her mother folded her arms across her bosom. "Tahlia Ann Armstrong, you better start talking."

"Come to my office." Tahlia led them toward the back offices. They passed Faith on the way.

"Hello, Mrs. Armstrong."

"Hello, my dear." Sophia gave Faith a hug. "So great to see you again." Tahlia had had Faith over for dinner at her mother's, and the two women had hit it off famously.

"You, too," Faith replied.

When they were behind closed doors, her mother stared back at her in anticipation. "Well, I'm waiting, young lady."

Tahlia stared back at her mother. Even at forty-six, her mother was still a knockout in her book. Her brown skin was bright and clear with no signs of aging. Meanwhile, thanks to her schedule as a RN, her mother was constantly on the go, keeping her body fit and trim—although you couldn't tell from the baggy jeans and tunic she wore now.

Now that Tahlia had a little money, she and Kaitlynn would have to take their mama on a mommy makeover. In the meantime, she responded to her mother. "I didn't exactly tell you the whole truth a few days ago."

"What did you leave out?"

"Well… In addition to leaving me this place, Arthur Knight gave me two percent ownership in Knight Shipping."

Sophia jumped up from her seat. "He did what?"

"Mama, please sit down."

"How can I sit down? Do you have any idea what that stock is worth?"

"I've some idea, but listen, there's more," Tahlia continued, taking a seat. When she did, her mother did the same.

"So there's a catch?" asked her mother, reaching out for her hand. "What is it?"

"I'm the deciding vote between Maximus Knight and his illegitimate brother, Lucius Knight."

"Oh, dear," her mother exclaimed. "I've seen the news reports about their father. But how did you get involved? Why would he put you in the middle?"

Tahlia shrugged. "I don't know, Mama. I think Arthur thought I'd help bridge the gap between them. You know how much I believe in family. I mean, look at the three of us and how tight we are. I think Arthur thought I could do the same for his family."

"That's a tall order," her mother replied. "I've seen the news reports. Up until recently, Lucius Knight was a bachelor playboy, but I believe he's engaged now, yes?"

Tahlia nodded. "I met his fiancée, Naomi. She's amazing and so talented. She started Brooks & Johnson."

"I love their products." Her mother touched her cheek.

"Mama, that's not the point," Kaitlynn intervened. "I don't trust Maximus. I don't put him above using Tahlia to get his own agenda through."

"I disagree. If you got to know him, he's a really nice guy," Tahlia stated. "We had dinner the other night, and he invited me to tour Knight Shipping and he invited Lucius."

"And whose suggestion was that?" Kaitlynn raised a brow.

"His," Tahlia responded. "But listen, until he does something to make me think otherwise, I should give him the benefit of the doubt. Isn't that right, Mama? You've always taught me to see the good in people."

"That's right, sweetie," her mother said. "You should, but you also need to be cautious. You wear your heart on your sleeve."

"I'm surprised that's still possible after Paul," Kaitlynn replied.

Tahlia frowned at her sister's mention of her exboyfriend, Paul Archer. "Did you have to bring him up?" They'd dated on and off for the better part of five years. Paul was the only serious relationship Tahlia ever had and the only man she'd ever loved. It had been hard accepting that they weren't meant to be like her parents.

It had been love at first sight when Sophia and Darryl Armstrong had met in the hospital. Her father had been a promising surgical resident who could have gone on to do great things, but his life had been snuffed out way too soon. Tahlia had always wanted a love like that one day. She'd thought she and Paul were meant to be, but in the end she'd learned they didn't want the same things. She wanted to be a wife and mother, and Paul didn't even want kids. When she'd been late and thought she was pregnant, even though she hadn't been, it had cemented that their relationship was doomed, and they'd parted ways soon after.

"I'm sorry, sis," Kaitlynn apologized when Tahlia's expression became downcast. "I just don't want a repeat of Paul. You and Maximus, Max, whatever he calls himself, are on two different playing fields. It's best you don't get your hopes up for something more."

"Why shouldn't I shoot for the stars?" Tahlia asked. "Unlike Paul, I knew the moment I saw Maximus that we'd have a connection."

"Did he realize that?"

"No," Tahlia admitted with a frown, "but he may now. Last night at dinner, I could have sworn he was going to kiss me."

"Tahlia, really, must you always have your head in the clouds?" her mother asked. "I'm sure a man like Maximus is taken."

"You don't think I can catch his attention, either?" Tahlia inquired. "Thanks a lot, Mama."

"It's not that, sweetie. Sometimes, you're a little too optimistic."

"You're wrong," Tahlia replied. She hadn't imagined that Maximus wanted to kiss her. She'd just put her foot in her mouth by including Lucius. But it was Arthur's dying wish that his sons get along and run Knight Shipping. So Tahlia had to do everything in her power to see that happen. She owed it to Arthur.

And she was positive that Maximus Knight was interested in her, and she couldn't wait to see him again.

"Tahlia Armstrong and Lucius Knight are here to see you, Mr. Knight," his assistant, Elena Masters, advised him from the intercom on Friday afternoon.

Maximus pressed the speaker button. "Thank you, Elena. Tell them I'll be with them in a minute." Then he sat back in his executive chair and took several deep breaths.

He was happy to see Tahlia again. Unfortunately, the request came along with an annoyance: Lucius. He would have turned Tahlia down immediately when she'd asked, but if he did, he would have raised a red flag. He needed Tahlia to be pliable, and the only way to ensure her cooperation was to act like he was keeping an open mind when it came to Lucius, when that was far from the case.

Rising from his chair, Maximus walked to the double doors of his office and opened them. His gaze immediately went to Tahlia, who sat on the sofa looking delicious in a bohemian-style crinkle skirt and tank top covered by a black blazer rolled up to her elbows. He assumed this was her twist to make it professional.

Meanwhile, his brother, Lucius, who was at least two inches taller than him, stood in what Maximus knew was a designer suit because he had the exact same one, although thankfully he wasn't wearing it now. Lucius sported his signature crew cut, mustache and goatee. And he was talking to Elena and had the poor girl blushing several shades of red.

He and Lucius couldn't be more different. Lucius was all flash and liked to be the life of the party, or so he'd heard, while Maximus was much more reserved and liked to observe and view the lay of the land before engaging. Their only similarity was the fact that they shared the same taste in clothing.

"Lucius." Maximus came forward, extending his hand.

"Aw, here's my little bro," Lucius said when Maximus came forward, but instead of accepting his handshake, Lucius drew Maximus into an awkward and unwanted hug. Maximus glanced at Tahlia from the sofa, and she was beaming at the contact. He tried not to recoil as he lightly patted Lucius on the back and pulled away.

"That really wasn't necessary," Maximus whispered.

"Of course it was." A faint light of amusement twinkled in his dark eyes. "We're brothers."

"I'm so glad you could join us, Lucius." Tahlia stood to her feet. "Max." She inclined her head toward him.

"Max, is it?" Lucius glanced in her direction, and his

brow rose. "It's like that now? How long have you know him, Tahlia? All of a week? Did I miss something? Do I get to call you Max now, too?"

Maximus forced himself to be polite when he'd like nothing more than to wring his older brother's neck. He was purposely stirring the pot, trying to rile him up, but Maximus was used to loud, overbearing men like Lucius and knew how to handle them.

"That's right," Maximus responded. "Tahlia and I have been getting to know each other." He gave her a wink and watched her eyes brighten at the action. "But no, I'd prefer you call me Maximus. Unless you'd like me to call you Luke or maybe Lucifer."

At that comment, Lucius howled with laughter. "I like you, Max." He slapped Maximus's shoulder. "You've got a sense of humor. Why don't you lead the way and show us *our empire*."

Maximus seethed inwardly but started walking down the hall. He led them through the executive offices first and then showed them the different departments on several floors before eventually ending in the shipping yard. This had always been his favorite place as a child even though it could be dangerous with all the cranes and shipping containers on the move. Tahlia asked a lot of questions throughout, but Lucius was silent, taking it all in. Knight International, Lucius's company, specialized in technology, not shipping. Maximus hoped he could see that he was out of his element.

"Looks awfully tight," Lucius commented as he peered at the shipping yard filled with cargo containers.

"Yes, it is," Maximus replied, surprised at his insight. "Expansion is the next logical step if we want to compete in the Port of Los Angeles with the other major players. If you didn't know it already, it's the largest port in the US."

Lucius rolled his eyes. "And I assume you're already looking at the feasibility and finances on moving forward?"

"Of course.

"Good. I look forward to seeing it in the future."

When the tour was over and they were headed back to the main building, Lucius commented, "This is quite an operation you have on your hands, Maximus." Gone was his previous arrogance about *their empire*. If he wasn't mistaken, Maximus had gained his older brother's respect.

"Thank you."

"Are there any major decisions that have been tabled given Arthur's death that you need Tahlia and me for? I assume you can handle day-to-day operations."

"Yes, of course," Maximus stated testily. "I've been president for the last two years and am quite capable of running things."

"I know that," Lucius responded. "It's clear Knight Shipping is in excellent hands. I only meant that if we—" he glanced at Tahlia "—could be of any assistance, we're here."

"There's a board meeting next month and we'll be discussing expansion options," Maximus responded, "but until then, I've got it."

Lucius stared at him long and hard as if debating his next answer, but then he just said, "Of course you do." He turned to Tahlia. "Tahlia, it's been a pleasure. Thank you for the invitation." He glanced at Maximus when he spoke. Lucius knew there was no way in hell he would have ever purposely invited him to tour the facilities. He glanced again at Tahlia. "Be careful of this one, though. He's real smooth." Then he looked back at Maximus. "Max, I'm sure we'll be speaking soon. Take care, little bro." He ruffled Maximus's curls and walked toward his car.

Tahlia was silent beside Maximus as he patted his hair back into place. He didn't appreciate the constant reminders that Lucius was the oldest and, in fact, could have been the heir to Knight Shipping if he'd been acknowledged as Arthur's son. As much as he hated it, Maximus would always be Lucius's younger brother, but did he have to mess his hair up?

"Max, I'm sorry about Lucius," Tahlia replied. "He's been baiting you all day with the bro comments and calling you Max. I'm sorry I extended the invite."

"Don't be, it's not your fault he was being a complete and utter jerk." Maximus turned to face her. When he did, he saw concern was etched across her beautiful features. "Really." He touched her shoulders. "I'll live."

"I know." She gave him a half-hearted smile. "You didn't rise to the bait."

He shook his head. "I learned a long time ago to be coolheaded and to not react, because isn't that what he expected?"

"And where did you learn not to show your emotions?"

"Ah, Tahlia, we're not getting into this discussion now," Maximus responded.

"When, then?" she asked boldly.

Maximus walked up to her until he was so close he could smell the shampoo she'd used that day. It smelled of lemon and lavender. "When would you like?"

He heard the breath hitch in her throat, saw her pupils dilate at his nearness. "I would imagine you'd want to keep your distance, given Lucius's warning to be wary of me."

Her lips thinned. "I make my own judgments."

"And what have you decided about me?"

"That I can trust you," she said, and then she added, "For now."

He studied her. He was getting to her. "Join me for dinner tomorrow night. I have a charity function."

Tahlia shook her head. "I can't, but if you'd like to share a meal, I'm free on Monday night. And I know just the place. I'll text you the address."

Seconds later, she was gone, leaving Maximus to wonder who was playing whom.

Chapter 5

Maximus's weekend was super busy. He attended a charity dinner with his mother on Saturday night and was now meeting up with Griffin on Sunday for their weekly racquetball match. It had always been an outlet for him when he needed to relieve some stress, and today was no different.

After the tour on Friday ended with Lucius and Tahlia, Maximus was preoccupied. Since his father's death, many decisions had to be made to keep Knight Shipping running. Now that he knew Lucius and Tahlia wouldn't be looking over his shoulder every five minutes or expecting a report, Maximus was free to make them. Lucius had even been open to the idea of expansion, though he didn't yet understand what that might entail. So it was up to Maximus to put together the best prospectus he could to convince Lucius, the businessman, that going public was in the company's best interest. But even if Lucius wasn't on board, Tahlia's vote would give Maximus the majority vote he needed to take Knight Shipping public.

Business decisions came easily, but another, more

personal one stood heavy on his mind, and that was whether he should continue on this quest to seduce Tahlia. He'd come up with the idea after he'd been steaming mad after the reading of his father's will, but now that he had time to think about it, he was beginning to question its legitimacy. Tahlia was gorgeous and had an inherent kindness that didn't lend itself to his machinations. But Maximus couldn't figure out any way around getting her vote, except appealing directly to her sensibilities. If she was interested in him, cared for him, it could sway any potential vote his way.

"Max, get your head in the game," Griffin said when a ball flew past Maximus's ear.

"Sorry, Griff." Maximus returned his focus to the game and got in position. Within seconds, another ball was coming at him, and this time he hit it with such force that it went sailing across Griffin's head.

Griffin glared at him. "What the hell was that?"

"Playing ball. Now stop your whining and let's get on with it."

An hour later, they were in the locker room having just finished up their match. Griffin had beat him by a point, 5 to 4. It hadn't been Maximus's best game because deep down he'd been thinking about Tahlia. Her lustrous black hair that hung in soft waves past her shoulders. Her big brown eyes. Or maybe it was those kissable lips that he knew were aching for him to kiss them.

"You let me win," Griffin said as they dressed after showering.

Maximus frowned. "Why would you say that?"

"Because you're distracted."

"You should take the win, Griff. You know I don't like to lose, and you might not ever get another chance to gloat." He'd already donned a pair of khaki trousers and was buttoning up a casual shirt.

Griffin shrugged as he pulled on his jeans. "I want to beat you when you're at your best, not when you're preoccupied with your family business or your beautiful new partner."

"Lucius?" Maximus said with a smirk. "I certainly wouldn't call him beautiful. Arrogant would be more like it. The other day during our tour, the jerk tried to rile me by calling me little bro and Max."

His friend chuckled. "Oh, I bet that really got your goat," he said, pulling on his polo shirt. "But you know good and well who I'm talking about."

"Tahlia."

"Of course," Griffin replied as he slipped on his shoes. "Have you followed through on your intent to seduce the woman in the hopes she'll part with her shares or vote with you?"

"And? What if I were?"

"I would tell you I think it's a bad idea. I know you have a way with women, but say you do seduce her. Who's to say that the relationship won't go sour and Tahlia votes against you anyway for spite? There's no guarantees this will play out exactly how you envision. Surely, there must be another way," Griffin said. "Some legal maneuver you can use to get Lucius out of the company. Has it even been confirmed that he's Arthur's son? Force him into a paternity test. You could drag this out in court for years."

"Only in the end to have to share the power with him after I've royally pissed him off?" Maximus asked. "No." He shook his head. "My way is better. If I can get Tahlia on my side or convince her to sell me her shares, it's the better method."

"If you say so, but you're treading a very fine line, my friend," Griffin said.

"I know that," Maximus said. But Tahlia was also a grown woman who could make her own choices. He'd heard Lucius warn her about him. She could choose to ignore his advances and he'd be back to square one. Ultimately, it was her decision.

"All right. When the script is flipped, don't say I didn't warn you," Griffin said and finished tying up his shoes.

"Don't sound so ominous," Maximus responded. "I can handle this."

Tahlia paced the sidewalk as she pulled the collar of her wool peacoat around her neck. It was a chilly Monday evening, and she was freezing her bones off as she waited in front of the homeless shelter where she and Maximus would be serving dinner tonight. Thanks to her mother's altruistic spirit, she'd always made sure Tahlia and Kaitlynn understood just how lucky they were when others were less fortunate. And so, she'd made sure her girls volunteered in some capacity throughout much of their teens. Now, into adulthood, Tahlia had continued giving back to her community, and serving dinner each week was just a small way for her to do so.

She hadn't told Maximus exactly where they'd be going for dinner tonight. She'd only texted him the address. As vehicles passed her by on the street, she looked out for his Bugatti. It would be very conspicuous in this neighborhood. Tahlia wondered if he'd even get out of the car or whether he'd pull up to the curb and tell her to hop in before driving her someplace more upscale.

But Tahlia planned on digging in her heels. Tonight was a test if Maximus was truly serious about wanting to spend time with her and not using her as her sister Kaitlynn suggested, as did Lucius, who'd warned her to be careful. And Tahlia was curious whether Maximus would pass it.

Instead, he pulled up alongside the curb at 6:00 p.m. on the dot in a Mercedes-Benz rather than his blue Bugatti sports car. He was nothing else if not prompt as he exited the vehicle looking handsome in a wool coat and scarf wrapped around his neck.

He smiled at her as he approached, but it faded once he glanced at the building. Then he looked in her direction. "Interesting choice for dinner."

"You don't mind, do you?"

Maximus shrugged. "It's ladies' choice. So let's get out of this cold." He motioned for her to walk ahead of him.

Once inside, the shelter was a bustle of activity as the staff prepared for the dinner rush. While they removed their coats, Tahlia allowed herself a few moments to take in Maximus. He'd clearly just come from work because he'd removed his suit jacket and wore a dress shirt, slacks and a tie, and here she was having him serve dinner in his designer duds to the homeless. She was sure he probably wanted to wring her neck, but he was a good sport and quickly dispensed with his tie and slid it into his pants pocket.

Tahlia was still pulling off her coat when Maximus came over to help relieve her of it. "Thank you." She glanced behind her.

"You're welcome."

Then he took both their coats and followed her into

the large room. Patrons were already lining up in preparation for dinner service. "C'mon." Tahlia inclined her head. "I'll show you where we can put up our coats." She walked with purpose toward the center's director, who was in charge of volunteers. The older woman smiled on her approach.

"Tahlia." The director gave her a quick hug. "It's so good to have you with us again." She glanced behind Tahlia at Maximus. "And who did you bring with you today?"

Maximus stepped forward and extended his hand. "Maximus Knight."

"It's a pleasure, Mr. Knight." The director shook his hand. "It's so great to have someone with your reputation helping out today. Let me show you where to put your things, and then I'll put you to work. With tonight's cold temperatures, we'll have a full house tonight for dinner."

"Lead the way," Tahlia said.

Fifteen minutes later, Tahlia and Maximus were outfitted with aprons, gloves and large spoons to help serve the food that was spread across several rectangular tables. At least a dozen volunteers were milling about and either serving food or on cleanup detail. Tahlia had signed them up for meal service.

Once the lines opened, patrons came past their table, and she and Maximus added spoonfuls of mashed potatoes and green beans to go along with the meat loaf already on their plates. It didn't take long for them to find a rhythm and to keep the steady line moving. Tahlia was sure this was the first time Maximus Knight had ever served anyone, but he was taking it in stride.

"Enjoying yourself?" she asked, glancing in his direction.

He offered her what seemed like a genuine smile. "Actually, I am. I can't say I've ever served the homeless on a date before, but yes, I am enjoying myself."

"Is that what this is?" she asked, her pulse speeding up. "A date? I thought we were just two business partners having dinner."

His eyes swept over her face, surveying her, then he leaned down to whisper in her ear. "You know it's a date." Then he served the next patron, and all Tahlia could do was stare up at him. The implication sent waves of excitement surging through her. She'd hoped it was a date, but having the confirmation caused an invisible warmth to wrap around her insides, which already felt like mush whenever Maximus was near.

The next patron was standing in front of her, and Tahlia had to look away from Max and remember why she'd come: to help others. They continued serving meals until nearly 8:30 p.m., when the director came over and allowed several of the volunteers to take a break and have dinner themselves.

"You don't mind having dinner here?" Tahlia asked when she and Maximus moved from the other side of the table to stand in line with the patrons. She handed him a paper plate.

"Not at all," he responded, accepting the paper plate. "I enjoy helping others, and if I get to spend time with you in the process, it's a bonus."

He delivered the line so smoothly, Tahlia was so flustered one of the patrons had to gently remind her to keep the line moving. Once she and Maximus had filled their plates, they sat at one of the picnic-style tables in the main hall with their now-loaded plates of meat loaf with all the fixins. Tahlia wondered what

Maximus was thinking as he sat across from her with a faint glint of humor in his eyes. *Is this how he envisioned our first date?*

Maximus stared at Tahlia. His dark eyes pierced her brown ones, and they sparkled when she deduced his obvious interest in her. If he was honest, he'd been eager to see Tahlia again after the tour and was curious as to where she would select to have dinner for their first date. He'd never in his wildest dreams imagined she'd take him to a homeless shelter for a meal. He glanced down at the less-than-appealing entrée.

But he had to hand it to Tahlia. She had spunk. Not many people could surprise him, and Tahlia had. She'd offered him a glimpse into a cause near and dear to her heart. Because of it, he intended to write a check later and give it to the shelter director. Maximus liked what he saw on the inside as well as the outside. Tonight, she was wearing a sweater dress that showed off her fine hips and shapely thighs along with boots that covered her calves. Despite the fact that she was covered from head to toe, Maximus was just as turned on as if she wore a minuscule bathing suit. He could only imagine how she'd fill out a bikini.

Tahlia was a breath of fresh air in his otherwise mundane life. Up until now, his life had been about achieving the lofty goals his father had set for him. But once he'd achieved one, it had never been enough and he'd set another one, a higher goal, until eventually his life had become so structured, he'd forgotten what it was like to just have fun.

Tahlia offered him that and so much more.

He wanted her.

And as he regarded her, he found a joyous satisfaction in knowing she was studying him just as much. She wanted him, too. He wanted this feeling to last, so he would take their relationship slow until she was finally in his bed.

"Why are you still single?" Maximus suddenly asked.

Tahlia frowned. "Where did that come from?"

"A woman as beautiful as you should be taken, so why are you on the market?"

"I could ask you the same thing," she responded, forking some meat loaf and plopping it in her mouth.

"Then I would answer and tell you that up until now I didn't really make time for activities outside of work."

"And now that's changed?" She quirked a brow.

"I'm not answering until you share your story," Maximus responded.

Tahlia shrugged. "All right, if you must know, there was someone once. Paul was his name, and I fell hard for him only to find out that he wanted a casual relationship and wasn't interested in a long-term commitment that came with marriage, kids and the white picket fence."

"His loss is my gain," Maximus responded. The man was a fool if he didn't realize what a gem Tahlia was. "And to answer your question, yes, circumstances have changed for me and I'm suddenly interested in extracurricular activities."

Tahlia blushed, and Maximus made a gallant effort to eat the meal in front of him and dug into the meat loaf. It wasn't the worst meal he'd ever had. And he'd do it for Tahlia to show her he wasn't some overprivileged rich kid who couldn't eat with those less fortunate.

"How's the meat loaf?" Tahlia asked with a smirk.

"Not bad."

"C'mon, Max," she said and laughed. "I know you'd

much rather be at some fancy restaurant having a chef-prepared entrée along with a bottle of expensive wine or something."

Maximus put his fork down. "Of course I would, but tonight was your pick. Next time, it'll be my choice."

"Next time?" She raised a brow and tried to hide a smile. "Who said there'd be a next time? I don't recall being asked."

"Then allow me to remedy that." Maximus reached across the table and laid his hand over Tahlia's. A surge of heat bloomed between them, and he could almost feel her skin heat up along with his. "Tahlia, will you go out with me on Saturday night?"

She gave him a genuine smile. "I'd love to."

"See, that wasn't so hard, was it?" he asked, not removing his hand. He noticed that she was shifting in her seat because he hadn't let her go.

"N-no, it wasn't." She tried unsuccessfully to slide her hand from his grasp, but instead, he linked his fingers with hers, without a thought to where they were or who was looking at them. He leaned across the table and did what he'd been wanting to do since she'd walked into the family estate for the reading of his father's will: he brushed his lips softly across hers and kissed her in the middle of the dining hall.

It was the lightest of kisses and it didn't last nearly as long as he would have liked, but eventually he sat back down across from her and looked at her. Her eyes were hooded with desire, making Maximus rethink his decision to take their relationship slow. But he didn't have time to think too long, because the room erupted with clapping.

Apparently, his little kiss had caught everyone's attention. Tahlia was embarrassed, and he watched her cheeks flush pink. There was a certain innocence to Tahlia that beguiled him. A woman of her age had to be experienced, but yet she appeared so sweet and genuine. Would his plan ruin that spark in her?

Tahlia had been unprepared for their first kiss. Sure, she'd wanted it from the moment she'd laid eyes on Maximus at the crowded gallery opening a year ago, but the reality was so much more than she could ever have imagined. She'd reacted strongly to his whisper of a kiss, and it hadn't even been a full-blown attempt. What would it feel like when Maximus lost control and kissed her with abandon?

Since she didn't like being the center of attention, Tahlia rose from the picnic table and reached for Maximus's plate. "You ready to go?" she asked. She didn't like that several people were openly staring at them. Perhaps ready for more of a show?

"Are we done?" he queried.

"I'll check with the director, and if we're no longer needed, we can scoot out."

It turned out they were needed and ended up staying another hour to finish up dinner service, and to her surprise, Maximus helped with some of the cleanup in the kitchen. It was well after 10:00 p.m. when they returned to the director's office, where she'd locked up their coats and her purse. Maximus helped Tahlia into her coat.

"This was really awesome," Maximus said. He spun her around and, to her surprise, began buttoning her coat.

"I can do it," Tahlia said, halting his hands with her own.

"I want to make sure you're warm," Maximus said, brushing her hands aside as he continued his task.

Tahlia looked down. Didn't he know she was not only warm, but she was also on fire from his touch? She hadn't recovered from his earlier kiss, and being in this confined space with Maximus was playing havoc on her senses. Her heart was already beating an erratic rhythm.

"Tahlia, look at me." Maximus's voice was husky with desire.

She met his eyes with hers, and they scanned her face slowly and seductively. And when his gaze slid downward to her lips and he lifted his thumb to caress them, her pulse quickened. Maximus tilted her chin upward with a finger to inch her closer to him. Tahlia knew what was coming next, and there was no hesitation on her part. She twined her fingers into his curly hair at the back of his head as she'd been longing to do. Sweet relief flooded her as he hauled her against him, bent his head and closed his mouth over hers.

This kiss was different from the one in the main hall. That had been a chaste peck in comparison with this one—his mouth claimed hers with skill and precision. His mouth possessed hers fully and deeply, so she kissed him back with all the passion she'd held inside her for this man. She didn't care that she was revealing her deep-seated need for him. Tahlia only knew that in the moment she had to give her desire free rein. She allowed him to push her against the office wall so he could have his way with her. She parted her lips, allowing his tongue to access the warm recesses of her mouth.

It was impossible to fathom the tumultuous emotions that he aroused in her. Maximus was an attractive and powerful man, and he easily swept away any barriers she had around herself as he intently discovered every sensual part of her mouth. His was a mission of discovery. But could he know that he'd been the man of her secret dreams and whom she'd fantasized about kissing?

She ran her hands over the bunched muscles of his upper arms that strained against the fabric of his shirt as he kissed her again and again, over and over. His lips were warm and firm in an unhurried exploration that drugged Tahlia's senses and apparently his, too, because she heard a groan from deep in his throat. She was no longer herself either, but a mass of needs wrapped around this one man.

When he lifted his head and stared down at her, his eyes were clouded. "Christ, Tahlia!" he whispered. "You're so darn eager. Do you know what a turn-on that is?"

Tahlia shook her head, and her cheeks flooded with color. She was equally as turned on. No other man had kissed her with quite the same intensity or fervor that Maximus had just now, not even Paul.

Slowly, he released her, and Tahlia had to right herself to keep from falling. She felt weak in the knees from his kisses. She watched him suck in a deep breath as he, too, tried to get a hold of his senses. After a few minutes, she dared to look at him and saw a look of blatant hunger lurking in those brown depths.

"I should walk you to your car."

She nodded. "All right."

They left the shelter and within a few moments were outside in the blistering cold. The chill would certainly help cool Tahlia down after Max's heated kisses. He grasped her hand, and they held hands all the way to her car. When they reached it, she turned to him. "I had a good time tonight."

"So did I." Maximus nodded. "And I'm looking forward to Saturday night. But first I need something to hold me until then."

And before she knew it their kiss had resumed, and this time his mouth not only searched hers, he conquered it. His mouth crushed hers, holding her firmly in place. The kiss was deep, raw and all-consuming. When he finally let her go, he had to open the car door and help her inside. She needed the assistance because she trembled with blooming need inside her for more. But Maximus didn't push. Instead, he seemed content to take it slow. Tahlia just hoped she didn't go up in flames in the meantime.

Chapter 6

Kisses. Sweet kisses. Tahlia. That, or should he say she, was all Maximus could think about last night. Thinking of her had kept him up half the night. How she'd tasted, how she responded, how much further he could have gone if...

"Maximus, darling, where have you been hiding yourself?" his mother inquired the next morning at the kitchen's breakfast nook. He had a place in town, but since his father's death he'd been spending time at his mother's mansion. She said it made her feel better.

"I've been busy, Mother." Why did she have to interrupt his most delicious daydream?

"I hope finding a way to overturn your father's will," she responded. "I mean, really? I can't believe he gave away half the company to Lucius. The rumors are already starting to get out, you know, that you're not solely in charge."

"And how would those rumors get out, Mother? Have you been talking to the gossipmonger friends of yours at the country club?"

"Don't speak ill of my friends, Maximus," Charlotte Knight said. "They've been nothing but support-ive of me throughout this entire mess. You've no idea what I've had to face—the press reporting your father's affair, the media constantly hounding me, my friends being harassed for details. All the while you get to go to work with no repercussions."

Maximus sighed. He had been in his own world and internalizing how his father's will affected him and his dreams of expanding Knight Shipping, so much so he'd been neglecting his mother. She'd been hurt by all this, too, and deeply embarrassed by the scandal. Though some of it was of her own making. "I'm sorry you feel you're facing this alone. I know this must be hard on you."

"It is." His mother sniffed, and he reached inside his suit jacket for a handkerchief and handed it to her. "I never thought this revelation would ever see the light of day, much less that your father would betray me, betray you in this fashion. He promised me."

"What do you mean?"

"I didn't know about Jocelyn until nearly five years into our marriage. I'd always thought Arthur married me for love, so imagine my surprise when I found out there was another woman, another son."

"How did you find out?"

"He'd gone away to Europe one summer, and when he returned, something was different. I could see he'd changed. He was happier and lighter somehow. I'd thought the time away had done him some good and he'd returned reinvigorated for our marriage, but he wanted a divorce."

"What?"

She nodded. "The thing is, I was already pregnant with you. Arthur was torn between doing the right thing for one son and the right thing by *me, his wife*. He chose me, us—" she pointed at Maximus "—but I suspect he stayed with me because my father had died and I'd inherited a large sum of money. Arthur's ambitions got in the way of his ultimate one true love, Jocelyn."

"So he hated you, *me*," Maximus stated, "because he was forced to stay with us."

"Maybe he did."

"So he punished me because I wasn't Lucius? Because he gave him up?" And his mother punished him by not sharing Lucius's very existence with him. She'd never told him he had an older brother. Who knew what relationship they could have had if the adults in their lives hadn't been so selfish.

"Maximus." His mother reached across the table. "You mustn't think that way. Your father loved you. If there was anyone he hated, it was me because I threatened to take it all away from him and leave him with nothing if he ever left me."

Maximus rose from the table. Now he was angry with both his parents. "Give it whatever spin you like, Mother. Arthur Knight was not only selfish, but he was a coward for choosing the easy way out and not going after the woman and son he loved. Maybe if he had, we all would have been better off." He strode toward the door. "I'm going to work. Thanks for the chat."

All it had done was remind him that he deserved Knight Shipping. After all Arthur had put him through, it strengthened his resolve to get what was due him: Tahlia's shares. Knight Shipping was rightfully his. He and his mother had paid their entire lives for the privilege. He just hated that the only way to that end was through Tahlia.

* * *

"Someone is on cloud nine. What gives?" Faith commented when Tahlia drifted through the gallery throughout the day as if she were walking on air. Even though there was a lot of work to be done for an upcoming exhibit Bailey already had in the works before her ownership, Tahlia was ecstatic.

She wasn't even the least bit put off when one of their top customers had railed at her for getting the framing wrong on an order. It hadn't been one Tahlia had taken, but she'd promised the woman they'd have it corrected and couriered to her home. Her resolution had brought a smile to the customer, and she'd finally left satisfied about her purchase.

"I am happy," Tahlia finally said. "Why do you ask?"

"I don't know." Faith shrugged. "Maybe it has something to do with the enormous arrangement that came for you today."

Tahlia smiled, thinking about the large bouquet of roses and calla lilies that had arrived earlier that morning from Maximus. The card had read Can't Wait for Saturday. Neither could Tahlia. She'd been so giddy last night after sharing not one, not two, but three kisses with Maximus at the shelter.

She'd been so sure he would hightail it and run once he realized their dinner date was at a homeless shelter, but he'd surprised her with his fortitude. She'd received a call from the shelter director that Maximus had a sizable check delivered to the shelter just that morning. He also hadn't been as stuck-up as she'd thought and had been willing to lend a hand, including washing dishes. Just thinking about his large masculine hands in the hot bubbly soap, hands that roamed her body when he'd kissed her, caused Tahlia's skin to get heated.

"You're blushing," Faith said.

"Stop staring at me, then," Tahlia countered.

"Are you going to share details?" Faith asked. "You used to not mind sharing news about your dates." She followed Tahlia into the back office.

"This is different. Those men were merely warm-ups for the main attraction."

"Because it's Maximus Knight?"

Tahlia spun around. "How'd you know?"

"I saw the card. But you've never been this jumpy or secretive before."

Tahlia let out a sigh. "That's because I've never liked a guy as much as I like Maximus."

"The feeling is apparently mutual," Faith surmised. "Those flowers are gorgeous."

"Aren't they?" Tahlia couldn't help gushing. She felt like a teenage girl.

"When do you see him again?"

"Saturday night."

"I'm so excited for you, Tahlia," Faith said. "I know you've had a crush on him for a while now. I'm glad to see it's not one-sided anymore."

"No, it's not. It's definitely mutual."

"You're certain of this?" Maximus asked the highly recommended probate attorney he'd hired to go over his father's will. "There's no way I can contest its validity?"

The attorney shook his head. "Everything is in order here, Maximus. Robert Kellogg is a fine attorney. He would have made sure of it."

Maximus nodded. He knew it was a long shot, but he'd had to try to see if there was anything he could do before he continued taking drastic measures to get his rightful inheritance. His mind wandered to Tahlia and how happy she'd sounded when she'd called him a couple of days ago to thank him for the flowers he'd sent. He typically didn't do the flowers-and-candies thing with women he dated.

Usually, his female companions were on his arm for just one night to attend a function or an important dinner. But for Tahlia, he was willing to pull out all the stops and be her Prince Charming. Yet it had continued to niggle him that he had to use her for his own means, kind of like Arthur had used his own mother to start Knight Shipping. And as much as he hated his father's actions, in this instance the old adage applied. *Like father, like son.*

"Thank you again." Maximus stopped his pondering long enough to shake the attorney's hand and walk him to his office door. "I appreciate the effort."

"Wish I could have done something for you."

Maximus shrugged. There wasn't anything anyone could do, which was why he would continue his quest to seduce and ultimately bed Tahlia.

"I have great news," Tahlia said when she called Kaitlynn late Friday afternoon.

"Oh, yeah? What's that?" her sister asked from the other end of the line.

"I just scored VIP tickets to the Bruno Mars concert tonight."

"Get out. That show has been sold out for months!" Kaitlynn exclaimed. "So how did you… No, let me guess. The illustrious Maximus Knight got you tickets?"

"No." Tahlia shook her head even though Kaitlynn couldn't see her. "We're not scheduled to go out until tomorrow night."

"Well, how, then?"

"One of my clients was so happy with his pieces that he gave me tickets. Can you believe my luck?"

"I sure as heck can't. So I hope this call means you're taking me as your date."

"Even better," Tahlia replied. "I have four tickets. So *you* and *I* can bring a plus-one."

"Seriously? That's great, Tahlia. I'm just finishing up here and I need to call Jonathan to see if he'd like to come." Jonathan Baker was Kaitlynn's pseudo boyfriend, or in Tahlia's opinion her friend with benefits, but who was she to judge? "And you? I assume you're bringing Max."

"Maybe. I haven't asked him. What if he's too busy? It's short notice after all." They were just getting to know each other, and he could have other plans, even another date.

"How will you know if you don't ask him?"

"I don't know…"

"Don't be a wuss, Tahlia. You want the man to come don'tcha? So just call him up and see if he's free."

After Tahlia hung up with Kaitlynn, she placed her smartphone on the desk in her office and stared at it. She wanted to call Maximus, but it was spur-of-the-moment and she would be disappointed if he turned her down. In the end, she decided to take her sister's advice.

"What are you doing?" Tahlia asked when Maximus answered the phone several moments later.

"Working. Why?"

"Oh." She was crestfallen, especially by the short tone in his voice. It was near the end of the workweek, and she was hoping he'd tell her it was quitting time. Although they didn't have plans until tomorrow, she wanted to see him again and had just the excuse.

"Tahlia," he chided, "what is it? Did you have something in mind?"

"As a matter of fact, I do," she replied in a rush. "A client of mine was so happy with the pieces he purchased at the gallery that he offered me four tickets to the Bruno Mars concert tonight. My sister is coming with a date, and I know it's short notice and all, but I was wondering if you didn't have any plans for tonight if you might want to come?"

"So you're asking me out on a date?" This time there was a smile in his voice.

"And if I were?"

"The answer would be yes," Maximus responded. "What time shall I pick you up?"

"Since I'm the one taking you out," Tahlia said, "I'll be picking you up. And be ready at six." Since he didn't have time to go home and change, Tahlia arranged to pick him up at his office. Luckily for her, however, she had just enough time to close the gallery and run home for a quick shower.

"You don't mind closing up?" Tahlia asked Faith when she was heading for the door.

"Of course not. At least you have plans for Friday night other than sitting home with a movie and a bowl of microwave popcorn like me."

"That does sound divine."

"Not nearly as much as moving and grooving to Bruno Mars with Maximus Knight. Now go on." Faith shooed her out the office. "You'd better get a move on it. You don't have a whole lot of time."

An hour later, Faith was rushing out of her apartment and down the stairs to her VW Bug to pick up Max. She'd had just enough time to shower and slide on her favorite jeans, cropped tank top, denim jacket and boots. She'd decided to leave her hair down since Maximus seemed to enjoy running his hands through it the other night when he'd kissed her. After a touchup on her makeup and a quick spritz of perfume in all her secret spots, she was driving to Maximus's office.

She was sure it came as a surprise to him that *she* had offered to pick him up, but she didn't mind being the one in control for the evening. Maximus Knight was used to being in charge and having everyone fall in line. Tonight, he was on her turf and he would play by her rules.

Maximus exited his office bathroom after a quick change into khaki pants, a button-down shirt and a sports coat. He usually kept several changes of clothing at the office. He had to admit he was looking forward to the concert. It would be a change of scenery for him to do something other than work late on a Friday night. He actually had plans. A date. With Tahlia.

He smiled when he thought of her. The woman was sure full of surprises. Telling him that *she* would pick him up. If she wanted to be in charge tonight that was just fine with him. He would just take a back seat and let her do all the driving—literally.

He locked up his office and took the elevator to the lobby, arriving at 6:00 p.m. just as she'd instructed. He smiled when he exited the building and saw Tahlia leaning up against her old beat-up VW Bug. She looked like one of those pinup girls in the snug-fitting jeans she wore, crop top that revealed a hint of her belly button and a denim jacket.

It gave him all sorts of wicked ideas on what he'd like to do to her on top of it. But instead he said with a wry smile as he walked toward her, "Are you sure it's okay to get in that death mobile? You sure you don't want to ride in the luxury that is my Bugatti? It's just in the garage." He pointed toward the building.

"Ha, ha, ha," Tahlia feigned laughter. "No, we are taking my baby here." She leaned over to caress the hood of the car, and when she did, it gave Maximus a view of her generous backside, and without thinking about it, he smacked her on it.

"Max!" She popped upright. "What are you doing?"

He laughed. "I don't know. You just looked so good standing there... I—I couldn't resist." Maximus couldn't remember ever losing control and slapping a woman on her behind. It was completely out of character for him, but so was going to a pop concert.

"Well, in that case," Tahlia said, tossing her hair over her shoulder, "look all you want."

He watched her sashay to the driver's side of the car and give him a wink before hopping in. Tonight was going to be a fun evening.

Chapter 7

The tickets Tahlia procured came with a special parking pass, so when they arrived at the venue, they had a prime parking spot. "This is really nice," Maximus said, feeling somewhat awkward that he couldn't make it around to the driver's side to open her car door for her. But Tahlia didn't seem to mind. She'd already sidled up to him as they walked to the arena.

Maximus slid his hand in hers and they walked side by side to the box office, where her sister and beau were already waiting for them.

"Tahlia!" A beautiful albeit shorter version of Tahlia approached them with a tall gentleman sporting baggy jeans, sweater and a baseball cap. Her sister looked directly at him. "And you must be Maximus."

"Call me Max." But before he could finish the sentence she'd already hugged him and was turning to her companion. "Jonathan, I'd like you to meet…"

"Maximus Knight," Jonathan answered. "I've read a lot about you. You're considered the next big thing for black-owned businesses."

"I don't know about all that." Maximus laughed. "But I hold my own."

"Are you guys ready to go in?" Tahlia asked from his side, holding up the concert tickets. "Because I'm ready for some 'Uptown Funk'!"

They all laughed in unison, but Maximus completely missed the joke. What was "Uptown Funk"?

He soon learned after the foursome stopped at concessions for hot dogs, popcorn and beer and made their way through the throng of people to the front row on the floor. Maximus couldn't remember the last time he'd had a hot dog, much less a beer. Tahlia was getting him out of his comfort zone, and he liked it —he liked it a lot.

"So 'Uptown Funk' is a song," Tahlia told him once they were seated and munching on their dogs and swigging beer. "C'mon, don't tell me you've never heard of it."

Maximus shrugged.

"We really do need to get you of the house more," she said with a chuckle.

"I told you. I don't get out much," Maximus replied loudly over the roar of the prelude music. "Usually work, work, home and the occasional social function."

"That's no kind of life, Max," Tahlia yelled back. "I'm going to make it my mission in life to loosen you up."

"I'm open to ideas," Max said, eyeing her intently. He could think of a horizontal way that would loosen him up quite nicely, but it was still too soon to be thinking along those lines. If he came on too strong, Tahlia might think it was all about sex when it wasn't.

He was truly enjoying her company and everything she had to offer. When he'd first come up with the idea to seduce Tahlia, it had occurred to him that maybe their connection would merely be physical. But Maximus was learning that every minute he spent with Tahlia was one of his own self-discovery.

When the lights blinked, indicating the concert was about to start, Tahlia scooted closer to him, and Maximus used the guise of darkness to press a kiss on her soft lips.

Her eyes widened slightly, and she looked at him but didn't pull away. Instead, she allowed his mouth to cover hers hungrily as he explored hers more thoroughly.

When they finally parted, he heard someone yell, "Get a room!"

Tahlia laughed, blushing, and bumped her shoulder with his. Maximus couldn't recall a time when he'd felt this alive.

The night only continued to get better, and not just from the opening act and main attraction of Bruno Mars, but just by being with Tahlia. He fed off her intense energy. He wasn't much of a dancer other than the formal training he'd received to dance the waltz at social functions. But he loved the way Tahlia moved to the music, especially when a particularly good song came on. He liked it when she stood in front of him and he was able to wrap his arms around her. When her behind brushed his crotch as she swayed to the groove, Maximus felt his erection grow in his jeans.

He wasn't the only one who noticed. Tahlia turned behind her and gave him a wicked grin. Oh, she knew what she was doing to him. *The little minx!*

He would get her back real soon.

After the concert, the foursome filtered out of the arena. "That was a lot of fun," her sister, Kaitlynn, said. "But I'm not ready for the night to be over. Do you guys want to come out and hang?"

"Sure, what did you…" Tahlia began, but was interrupted by Maximus.

"No," Maximus stated, circling his arm around Tahlia. "We're going to call it a night."

"Okay, well, we're going to head out," Kaitlynn said. "I'll see you on Sunday at Mom's?"

"Absolutely." The sisters hugged while Maximus and Jonathan shook hands.

"It was great to meet you, Kaitlynn."

"You, too, Max. Don't do anything I wouldn't do." She winked at them as they walked away holding hands.

"So, did you enjoy yourself?" Tahlia asked, swinging their arms as if they were two small children to the lot where her car was parked in a reserved space.

"Yes, I did. I had a lot of fun, but I especially enjoyed watching you."

Tahlia paused midstep. "Me? Why?"

"I loved your inhibition and freedom as you danced and grooved, uncaring of what anyone else might think."

She shrugged. "Dancing is just a form of self-expression. You should try it sometime, Max, and not be so reserved. You have to be able to let yourself go."

"How about we start with this?" Maximus swung her in his arms, backing her up against the car so his entire body could cover hers and she could feel the erection she'd been teasing half the night. He ground the steel of his shaft against her, and she gasped. That was when his mouth moved over hers, smothering her lips, devouring their softness. She was shocked at Maximus's boldness, giving him the window he needed to break through the barrier of her lips and to invade her mouth with his tongue.

Tahlia groaned when he changed the pace from hungry, raw kisses to slow, gentle ones that were no less demanding as he cupped her breasts. Desire, hot and demanding, coursed through Maximus when she began rubbing against him, and he felt her breasts swell.

"Jesus, Tahlia!" He lifted his head as he nearly came undone. "You're killing me."

"You started it," she whispered, placing a feather-light kiss on his chin. "I think you wanted to show me you're not so reserved, right?"

He chuckled. "Mmm...I guess I did start it, but we can't finish it tonight, at least not here in this parking lot." Concertgoers and passersby were still walking to their cars, and they'd already given them quite a show.

"All right, I'll take you back to the office." Tahlia reluctantly disengaged from him. The car ride back to the Knight Shipping office crackled with sexual tension as memories of their sexual encounter in the parking lot stirred them. She was happy when the car came to a merciful stop in front of his building.

"I had a wonderful night," Max said, running his hand down the length of her arm. "And I can't wait for tomorrow night. Dress comfortably." He lightly caressed her cheek, and seconds later he was out of the car, leaving Tahlia feeling restless and oh so horny.

Tahlia excitedly waited for the doorbell to ring the following evening. She'd been ready for the last half hour and nervously pacing her one-bedroom apartment. She didn't know where they were going, only that Maximus had told her to dress comfortably.

She'd decided upon her favorite minidress that clung to her behind and teamed it with a black leather moto blazer and some ankle boots. Since it was a bit cool for a winter evening, she added a loose scarf to wrap around her neck.

Tahlia couldn't remember the last time she'd been this excited for a date, certainly not since Paul. She'd been cuckoo for Cocoa Puffs for him at the time, and he'd easily told her what she wanted to hear, but not Maximus. It surprised her just how different he was from what she'd expected. From afar, she would have thought him somewhat rigid, but so far he'd shown an amazing willingness to go with the flow. Tahlia had never been one to follow the crowd, and it was nice to know that Maximus could do the same.

When the doorbell rang, Tahlia didn't wait for him to come up. Instead, she rushed down the stairs and met Maximus on the first landing and threw herself in his arms. She buried her face in his throat and inhaled his magnificently masculine scent that was his alone.

"Hello, beautiful." When he brushed his lips across hers, it sent a shiver down Tahlia's spine. "Are you ready for a night of surprises?"

"Yes, I can't wait." She flashed him a grin.

On the drive to their mystery destination, Tahlia shared with Maximus her ideas and goals for the gallery. She wanted it to be a place for free expression and thought. A place where you could find the traditional and the unconventional. Maximus was all ears and gave her some sound advice on how best to achieve them. She was enjoying the conversation so much she didn't realize their destination until he stopped his Bugatti in the middle of a helipad.

"What are we doing here?" Tahlia exclaimed after Maximus had helped her out of his vehicle and she saw the helicopter with a pilot standing beside it.

"I'm taking you on a sunset tour of Hollywood. We're

riding in style, baby," Maximus said, grabbing her hand and leading her toward the helicopter. "C'mon."

In no time, Tahlia was strapped into one of two passenger seats and given headphones so she and Maximus could communicate, and then the pilot was taking off.

"Maximus, this is amazing," Tahlia said over the roar of the engine and wind as the helicopter soared in the air. She'd never done anything this thrilling in her entire life, and he was the reason for it. They took in all the sights Los Angeles had to offer, from the famous Hollywood sign to downtown Los Angeles to the Venice Beach boardwalk, celebrity homes, mountains of Malibu and the beautiful California coastline. Although it was dark, the lights of the city and Los Angeles skyline shone brightly.

When the exhilarating adventure was finally over, Tahlia and Maximus thanked the pilot. He'd given them a bit of history about each landmark they passed, making Tahlia want to do it all over again. She told Maximus so in the car on their drive to dinner.

"You outdid yourself," she gushed when they were on land. "I've never been in a helicopter before."

"No?" he asked with a smirk.

"I'm sure you have," she said, "no doubt to make important business meetings."

"But of course." He laughed. "That's how we moguls roll."

Tahlia playfully punched his arm. "You know, Maximus, I think I'm starting to like you." The moment she said the words aloud, she covered her mouth. Why did she always say whatever came to her mind?

Maximus took his eyes off the road long enough to say, "I'm starting to like you a lot, too."

Her heart took a perilous leap, and Tahlia swallowed

tightly, dropping her gaze to her trembling hands. With one hand on the wheel, Maximus grasped hers with his other and gave it a gentle squeeze. Tahlia could feel the blood surging through her fingertips from the simplest of actions, but it meant everything to her.

They ended up at Wolfgang Puck's restaurant at the Hotel Bel-Air. The food was delicious, the service impeccable and the company was everything Tahlia could hope for. Maximus was a lot funnier than she gave him credit for and regaled her with stories from his days at Harvard while Tahlia told him about growing up without a father.

"It must have been very hard for your single mother raising two girls on her own," Maximus said as they shared a dessert.

"It was. And at times we struggled," Tahlia admitted as she dug her spoon into the creamy mousse. "And it was in those moments that I missed having a father. But my mother gave me and Kaitlynn all the love we could ever need. I never for a moment doubted I was loved."

"I wish I could say the same," Maximus responded, "because all I've ever done is doubt my father. Did he love me? Did he not? He certainly wasn't one for showing it, so I guess I'll never really know."

Tahlia stared at him for several long beats. "I know he didn't show it, Max, but Arthur did love you. It may not seem like that now, but he told me how proud he was of you and your accomplishments. Everything that you've achieved. Please believe that."

Maximus's gaze darkened, and Tahlia could see how deeply her words were affecting him. "Thank you, Tahlia, and I know you mean well, but we're well past the point of my caring what my father thought of me."

Tahlia shook her head. "That's not true. I think you

need to hear it to believe it so you can make peace with him and with your older brother one day."

Maximus stared incredulously at Tahlia. He couldn't believe this was happening. That they were sitting here discussing his father as if he hadn't ripped his heart out of his chest when he'd given half the company to Lucius. It seemed so surreal.

"Tahlia, let's drop this topic of conversation, shall we?" Maximus said brightly. "Tonight was meant to be about you and me, not the ghosts of our past, present and future."

She smiled at his comment. "True, I just…"

She didn't get another word out because Maximus leaned toward her and brushed a featherlight kiss across her lips. He opened his eyes and glanced at her, and when she didn't resist him, he kissed her again, but this time he lingered, savoring the moment. When he finally pulled away, their breaths were both ragged.

"Maximus…"

"Do you have any idea how hard it is not to take you upstairs to one of these rooms and ravish you all night long?"

Tahlia inhaled sharply, and he could see that she, too, was struggling with what was the right move in this situation. They'd known each other only a couple of weeks, and although the attraction between them was strong, he wanted her to be sure before she went to bed with him. It had to be her choice. The fact that she didn't make a move or utter her consent made Maximus's decision easier. "I'll take you home," he said softly.

They were contemplative on the ride to her apartment, so much so that when they arrived, they both seemed equally shocked. "We've arrived," he said, turning off the engine.

"Yes, we have." But Tahlia made no move to go inside.

He twisted around, and his large hands grasped both sides of her face. "If you ask me in, you know what will happen."

She didn't speak. Instead, she wound her arms around his neck and brought his head down to her waiting lips. His entire body jolted at the contact, kicking him into high gear. Maximus pressed his lips to hers, and it was all over. In that moment, she was his, and he sealed it by sliding his tongue in her mouth and initiating a series of slow, drugging kisses, then deeper ones as he plundered her mouth.

Lust was jackknifing through him, and he couldn't resist pulling at her leather jacket so he could touch her. His hands roamed and his thumbs sought her nipples through the sparkling top. He squeezed them between his fingers and watched them bud for him. He so desperately wanted to taste them, taste her—he had an overwhelming need to be inside her.

Tahlia clutched at him, and a smothered sigh of longing escaped her lips. It caused Maximus to slow his passionate raid and to kiss a path from her lips to her throat, to her ears and back again to her lips. He didn't want their first time together to be a fevered coupling in a car. He wanted time to properly savor her.

"Tahlia, we have to stop," Maximus murmured. He pulled away from her and leaned his head against the headrest of his seat while he caught his breath. When he finally asserted enough willpower over his own wayward flesh, he looked at Tahlia. "Soon," he promised. "Soon you'll be mine."

Chapter 8

Maximus's words replayed in Tahlia's mind while she and her sister, Kaitlynn, took a yoga class midweek. Tahlia had hoped that the activity would ease some tension and allow her mind to rest, but all she could think about was how incredible it had been like to be with Max, how deliciously addictive he'd tasted, how thrilling it had felt to have his tongue mate with hers. She couldn't wait for the coming weekend because that was when they planned on seeing each other again.

It just seemed like the longest wait ever. Tahlia wasn't sure she could go the entire week without having him kiss her. Maximus had aroused her so much that his slightest move made her pulse quicken. She couldn't seem to control her reaction to him. He made her crave to be held in his arms, touched by him, such as when his fingers had skimmed her breasts and brought her nipples to peaks. She'd felt safe in his arms.

"Earth to Tahlia," Kaitlynn said, waving a hand in front of her as they wiped their sweaty faces from the workout in the locker room of their local fitness gym.

"Sorry, sis," Tahlia said and returned to the conversation.

"You've got it bad," Kaitlynn said. "I didn't think it was possible after Paul broke your heart, but Maximus Xavier Knight has you strung up tighter than the strings on a guitar."

"Does not."

"Does, too," her sister responded, "and I'm a bit worried. I saw you with him at the concert, and you seem awfully invested so soon into this relationship. Perhaps you should be taking this slower."

"We have been," Tahlia whispered, "so slow. We haven't even slept together."

Kaitlynn raised a brow. "You haven't? I would have thought that was a foregone conclusion, seeing how into him you are."

Tahlia spanked Kaitlynn's behind with her towel. "I'm very conservative, you know. I don't just sleep around. And, well, Maximus is being very patient. We're waiting for the right time."

"I sure hope that comes quick," Kaitlynn said with a laugh. "Otherwise, you're going to combust."

Tahlia rolled her eyes upward and then laughed herself. "You actually might be right. I didn't know it was possible to be this *horny*," she whispered so none of the other women could hear her.

"You—" her sister pointed to her "—need to take care of that, stat. When's your next date?"

"Saturday night."

"If I were you, I'd let him know in no uncertain terms that Saturday night is the night."

Oh, Tahlia intended to do just that. There was no way she could go through another night like last night. She'd actually ached between her thighs because she'd wanted him so much. It had taken every ounce of restraint not to drag him from the car and into her apartment building.

"And one thing, sis?"

"What's that?"

"Just be careful with your heart," Kaitlynn said. "I know you're an adult and everything. And you're feeling him all kind of ways, but remember at the end of the day, you're also business partners. There may come a time when you're on opposite sides of the fence and you'll have to decide where your loyalties lie."

Tahlia frowned. She hated that Kaitlynn was raining on her parade, but her sister had a point. Neither she nor Maximus had discussed exactly how a relationship between them would work, especially when it came to Knight Shipping. She'd been so caught up in the man that she hadn't given thought about the business since her tour with Lucius. And Maximus certainly hadn't brought it up during their dates together. He hadn't even mentioned the expansion he suggested during their tour. But surely, they wouldn't be put to the test that quickly. How bad could it really get?

Maximus was excited when Saturday finally arrived because he knew that tonight was the night. He would no longer push down his need to have Tahlia. Tonight he would unleash the passion he'd been restraining since they'd first met.

Since their date the previous Saturday, he'd made sure he had a steady diet of work, work and more work with an occasional stop for food, to work out and to enjoy his Sunday racquetball session with Griffin. When his friend had questioned him as to the status of his relationship with Tahlia, he'd remained mum and said it was progressing. He didn't need any recriminations at the moment.

Maximus figured if he kept busy, he'd keep his mind off Tahlia, but that lasted until only midweek. On Wednesday, he'd broken down and stopped by with lunch. He'd brought her and her assistant, Faith, salads to the gallery, and they ate in the conference room, all the while gazing at each other hungrily. His body was in tune to hers, eager to feed off her passion. Because when he touched her, her reaction was instant. Her responsiveness would only fuel his appetite in the bedroom, and there was no way he would be bored.

Oh, yes, tonight she would become his.

He'd planned a romantic evening ahead for them, ending with a stay at the bachelor pad he kept in downtown Los Angeles. It was his private retreat. He'd been staying at the estate since his father's death only because his mother had seemed so fragile without him. Though in his mind, she'd never really had his father's heart. It had gone to Jocelyn decades ago.

Maximus was dressed in his tuxedo and headed to the limousine parked outside the estate when his mother's voice stopped him on the steps leading to the foyer.

"Another evening out?" she inquired.

"Yes, and don't wait up. I'm spending the night at my place." He didn't wait to hear her response because he had somewhere to be.

Tahlia stared at herself in the mirror, impressed with the results she'd achieved. It was a miracle what makeup could do for you. She'd sprung for a treat and had her makeup and hair professionally done for her date with Maximus. Normally, she'd never have the money to spend on such an extravagance, but now that the gallery was hers, Tahlia figured she could splurge on a new look for tonight. When Maximus had told her to dress formally, she'd gone shopping. Now she was sporting a form-flattering gown and some strappy heels. She loved how the dress lifted her bosom and curved to her backside, giving her an hourglass figure.

He was right on time as usual, and her doorbell rang at 6:30 p.m. Tahlia reached for her small clutch and an overnight bag. She knew it was presumptuous as they'd not agreed that tonight they would take their relationship to the next level, but she suspected that Maximus was just as eager as she was to finally give in to the rampant lust that had colored their every encounter.

When she saw him, her heart did a somersault. He looked delectable in a black tuxedo with a silver bow tie. And he must have liked what he saw, because he whistled. He actually whistled when she came toward him.

"You look stunning!" He tucked her arm in his while his other grabbed her overnight bag. He didn't say anything about it. Instead, they walked to the limo, and once he'd helped her inside and given her bag to the driver, Max slid in beside her.

Tahlia was surprised at how nervous she felt given this wasn't their first date. She supposed it was because she'd made the decision to become intimate with him, and once sex entered the equation it changed everything.

"Relax." He reached for her hand and squeezed, but he didn't let go. He merely held it in his for the duration of the drive.

Tahlia began to suspect their destination as they climbed the hill and was pleased when the limo stopped and the driver helped her out of the car. They were at the Griffith Observatory.

"This place is spectacular."

"I know," Maximus said. "I've always loved the view, and since I know someone who works here, I've been able to arrange a little something special."

As they walked into the observatory, an older gentleman came toward Maximus. "Max, good to see you tonight."

"You, as well. Dennis Marshall, meet my girlfriend, Tahlia Armstrong."

Tahlia beamed inwardly. They'd never discussed titles, and although it was early on in the relationship, she was glad he felt that way. "Nice to meet you."

"As you know, I couldn't rent out the entire observatory to you, but we do have a terrace that's being refurbished thanks to your generous donation as a friend of the observatory. It's been set aside for you both. Follow me."

Dennis led them to one of the many terraces at the observatory. When they arrived, Tahlia was stunned to see a candlelit table for two set up along with a uniformed waiter and a harpist standing nearby.

She spun around to face Maximus. "You arranged all this?" No one had ever gone to this much trouble to impress her, and Tahlia had to admit she was blown away.

He shrugged. "For you, I'd do a lot more."

His breath was warm and moist against her face, and Tahlia's heart raced. She was truly touched that he would try to make this night memorable for the both of them. She didn't protest when he took her hand and led her to one of the seats. Instead, she settled back to enjoy the evening ahead, though it was hard to do because she couldn't tear her gaze from his face. He was so very good-looking and she was attracted to him.

Tahlia didn't know how she'd sit still without jumping his bones, but she did.

She enjoyed a delicious four-course meal that was one of the best she'd ever had as they talked about their week. Maximus shared with her bits and pieces about Knight Shipping and a new contract he'd landed. Not nearly as much as she would have liked, but they were taking baby steps. Meanwhile, Tahlia shared that she was working on her own art exhibit.

He grinned, clearly pleased with himself. "You're taking my advice."

She nodded. "I've always wanted to have one of my own, but after I got rejected by several galleries, I'd begun to wonder if I was any good."

"Don't let others' opinion sway you," Maximus said. "You're capable of great things, Tahlia. You just have to believe in yourself."

"I'm beginning to."

"Will you let me see what you're working on?"

His steady gaze bore into hers, and she nodded. "If you'd like me to."

"I would like that very much."

After dessert, Maximus pulled her into his arms and they danced to the strains coming from the harpist. Her arms moved of their own volition, clasping behind his neck as she melted into him. Because of it, she was conscious of where his warm flesh touched hers, and her skin tingled when his thighs brushed hers.

Eventually, she relaxed, sinking into his embrace. It was a magical night, and with the stars twinkling overhead, it was a night made for romance. More than that, Tahlia enjoyed being cradled in Maximus's arms as he rocked them back and forth. She could feel the evidence of his arousal pressed against her stomach. She could hardly believe that she was here in this moment with him, the man she'd dreamed about but never thought she'd ever meet. And now they would become lovers.

One of his hands stroked her cheek. "What are you thinking about?"

"Me. You. All of it," Tahlia answered honestly. She didn't know how else to be when she was around him. Whenever he was near, she was an open book, but Tahlia longed for the moment when Maximus wasn't so restrained. She wanted to see him completely lose control. Would he do so tonight when they made love for the first time? Would he allow himself to be vulnerable?

As if reading her mind, he cupped her face in his warm hands and kissed her deeply. Her tongue tangled with his, and Tahlia pressed herself against him, wanting every part of her body to be touched by him. When he lifted his head, his eyes were riveted on hers. She could hear his uneven breathing as he held her close. "Can I have you tonight? Will you be mine?"

"Yes."

Maximus's control was slipping. After Tahlia told him she would be his, it had taken every ounce within him to pull away from her so he could bring their evening at the observatory to a close. He thanked Dennis on his way out before they settled into the limousine so he could focus solely on her. All night he'd been mesmerized by her, from the soft peach color of her couture spaghetti-strap dress showing off the delicate slope of her shoulders to the sexy heels that added at least four inches to her height. She'd looked twice as sexy as she ever had.

As soon as the limo door closed, they reached for each other. Maximus had Tahlia underneath him in five seconds flat, and they began kissing, touching and caressing each other.

"You are so beautiful." He whispered a litany of praises as he tongued Tahlia's ear, and she responded by moaning and writhing on the limo seat. He could feel his erection swell in his tuxedo trousers. If she kept this up, it would be over with quickly.

"Tahlia, slow down, babe. We have all night."

And they did.

Tahlia had brought an overnight bag because she, too, had known that the time for waiting was over. Tonight, he wanted her hot and wet underneath him. If he could, he'd do it right now. He'd lift her dress up and skim his hands all the way to heaven, but he had to cool things down a bit. Slowly, he pulled them both upright until they were in the seated position.

Tahlia's hair was mussed and her lipstick barely visible because he'd kissed it clean off. By the end of the night, he intended to have her a lot more disheveled. In fact, he wanted her begging for him to come inside her.

As the limo came to a stop, Tahlia combed her fingers through her hair and he helped fix her dress back in place. He'd been desperate to taste her, so one shoulder strap had come down because he'd been kissing and nipping at the soft flesh. He exited the vehicle first and whispered to the driver to see that her bag was delivered to the penthouse. Then he helped Tahlia from the limo.

He curved her arm in his as they walked inside the building. He greeted the doorman with a terse nod and went for the penthouse elevator. He had his own private elevator that would take them to the top floor, where they would not be disturbed for the rest of the night.

Because that was exactly what it would take for him to satiate the desire he had for Tahlia.

All night.

* * *

Tahlia didn't notice much of Maximus's beautifully appointed penthouse when they arrived because they never turned on the lights. With the moonlight streaming through the windows, she spun around to face him. His gaze traveled over her face, searching her eyes. If he thought he'd find reticence, he wouldn't. Tahlia had never been surer of what she wanted. And she wanted Maximus.

He stepped forward, clasping her body tightly in his, and without a single word lifted her into his arms and walked straight to his bedroom.

She wanted this man. Oh, how she wanted him. And when he laid her down on the king-size bed, Tahlia reached up to draw him down to her.

Maximus tasted so good, so deliciously addictive, that Tahlia parted her lips and allowed his bold and daring tongue to do thrilling things to her mouth. It swirled and danced and played with hers, making her want more, much more of Maximus. Every part of her ached to be touched by this man, and she clung to him, wrapping her ankles around his, eager to be closer.

He lifted his head and looked down at her. His eyes were hazy with desire. "We should undress. I want to see you naked. Feel your skin on mine."

Tahlia didn't blush at his words. Instead, she untangled herself and began wiggling her way out of her dress.

"Here, let me help." Maximus's hands lightly brushed her skin as he lifted the silky fabric over her shoulders and head and dropped it to the floor. Tahlia wasn't wearing anything other than a strapless bra and bikini panties, and the look of unadulterated lust on Maximus's face made her feel desirable.

"God, you're beautiful…"

She smiled and reached behind her to unfasten her bra, but Maximus stopped her. "Let me…" He unclasped the unwanted garment and tossed it aside. His eyes feasted on her bare breasts.

Maximus reached out and cupped them in his palms. "I can't wait to taste you," he said, stroking her chocolate nipples. They puckered in response to his touch. "But you still have too many clothes on."

Tahlia leaned back on her forearms so Maximus could hook his fingers into the band of her panties and glide them down her trembling thighs. When she was completely naked, he peered down at her. His gaze riveted on her sex. Then he began stripping off his clothes.

Tahlia sucked in a deep breath as she watched him remove piece after piece of clothing. Maximus wasn't overly muscular like some men; his body was all lean muscle and sinew. And when he removed his pants and she got to see the most intimate part of him, she stared unabashedly at his big and powerful shaft. He was more beautiful than she could have ever imagined. She reveled in the knowledge that tonight he was *hers*. And vice versa.

When he joined her again on the bed, Tahlia couldn't wait to get her hands on him and began touching him everywhere she could, from the rippled muscles of his arms to his taut nipples to his flat, lean stomach, to his firm behind. She wanted all of it, all of him. He allowed her to explore him, barely touching her with only the slightest caress of his fingers. It didn't matter. He'd already lit a fire inside her from the moment they'd officially met.

And when his hands cupped her face and he kissed her slow and deep, Tahlia nearly whimpered with hunger. She was feeling so much. Having Maximus's lips, tongue and hands on her was *everything*. They were finally naked, their bodies touching, her breasts against his hard chest, hips and thighs tangled together. Tahlia laced her fingers through his curls, and as his kiss became more intense, her response became feverish to his searching tongue.

Maximus worked her mouth while his hands moved downward to tease her breasts with his fingertips. Her already sensitive nipples were aching for him, and he read her mind, his mouth leaving hers to find its way to where she needed him. He took her breasts in his hands, and his mouth closed over her nipple. He licked and teased her with featherlight flicks of his wet tongue before sucking on the hardened tip.

After leaving one breast, he moved to tease and coax a response from the other. His mouth continued its exploration as he made his way down her body, kissing and caressing her every nook and crevice. His hot mouth and searching fingers were blazing a trail of fire everywhere he went, striking a match to her need. All she could do was lie back, propped on her elbows, and watch him. Hunger was etched across his face as he skimmed his way down her entire body before stopping at her center.

"I can finally taste you properly," Maximus murmured as he hovered over her, and Tahlia held her breath in anticipation of what was to come. She was unprepared for the openmouthed kiss he placed there, and her hips jerked involuntary.

"Easy, baby," Maximus whispered, grasping her hips in his hands. "I've got you."

Tahlia was in disbelief that this handsome man's head was spread between her open thighs and was poised to give her more pleasure than she'd ever known. Tahlia arched her back, baring herself to him, so he could take all of her. But she wanted even more. "Please…"

He bent his head again, and the sensation of having his mouth on her caused Tahlia to tip her head back and moan. And when he slid a finger inside her to stroke her walls, she shuddered. His mouth and fingers didn't stop their exploration of her wet heat. It was such a delicious torment that Tahlia gave herself over to him.

"Oh, yes. Yes!" She let go, her hips rising to meet his searching tongue and fingers. And when she could take no more her, her muscles contracted, her body tensed and she climaxed.

Maximus slowed his actions as Tahlia's entire body felt sated. "I'm not done with you yet," he said as his hands slid up her torso to toy with her breasts again. "This was just the beginning."

As he looked down at her, Maximus had to admit he was enjoying every moment of Tahlia's first climax with him. He'd known she'd be this way, this responsive to him, his kisses, his touch, but she'd been completely uninhibited with him, and he wanted more. It surprised him that in a short amount of time, he'd come to care for her, want her. It had taken a supreme amount of patience for him not to beg her to let him come up last Saturday night, but he was glad he had. Because this was so much better. The buildup of their first time together had made him even more excited of what was to come.

He wasn't the only one ready for more. Now that she'd recovered, Tahlia was pushing his chest down until he was flat on the bed. She ran her hands across his chest. She bent her head and trailed a path of hot kisses all over his chest. He acknowledged her taking control by running his fingers through her hair. But when she came to his nipples and brushed her lips against one, he tensed.

He was going to be in trouble.

She teased his nipples with gentle flicks of her tongue, and every cell in his body came on fire. She stoked the flames. Her hot tongue moved from one nipple to the other, paying each equal homage. But she wasn't done with him yet. She continued worshipping his body, kissing his abdomen and stomach before going straight to the source of his inferno.

As she crouched on her knees, her long hair brushed his abdomen, and Maximus let out a long sigh of appreciation from deep within him. And when her small hands grasped his burgeoning shaft, Maximus nearly leaped off the bed. This fiery vixen had *him* quivering. His erection pulsed in her delicate hands, but she didn't shy away from him. Instead, she licked him.

Again and again, she licked the sides and bulbous head of his shaft, teasing him with light flicks of her tongue and then with bold strokes. His body responded, and he swelled even more in her hands, and that was when she took the crown into her mouth and sucked.

Sweet Jesus!

Maximus wasn't sure he could take it, but take it he did. In fact, he groaned, "More…"

And she gave him more, bobbing her head up and down his shaft, taking him even deeper into her mouth. Maximus was just a man, and she brought him to his knees as he came inside her mouth. Tahlia licked every bit of him up with her tongue, and when she raised her head and stared up at him, she asked, "Did you like that?"

Maximus's heart was pounding loudly in his chest

and his heartbeat had yet to return to normal. "You—you know I did."

She grinned mischievously. "Turnabout is fair play."

Maximus reached for her and pushed her back into the pillows. "Well, then, let's see who comes first next time."

Tahlia felt even more excited by Maximus's playful and provocative words. She'd taken charge, and he'd come undone just as he'd made her. It was powerful knowing the effect she could have on this man and that he was finally willing to be vulnerable with her, but she suspected they'd only just touched the surface on how deep their connection went. She watched as Maximus reached inside his nightstand for a foil packet and put on a condom.

Then he returned to her, and she parted her legs to make room for him so his mouth could plunder hers once more. He stilled and looked into her face, into her soul. Then he reached between them to ensure she was still wet and ready for the moment. She was and lifted her hips and felt him position himself, and then he kissed her just as he eased inside her.

Tahlia cried out, closing her eyes from the intensity—the feel of him. Her fingers caught in his hair at the unbearable pleasure of having him inside her. He paused while her body got used to his. She was trembling. So his arms encircled her, and he thrust in again, this time deeper, filling her.

Talia wanted him to lose control as he'd done a moment ago, so she began working her muscles around him. His eyes widened. So she worked them harder—it pleased her when he let out a hiss of air. She was getting to him. She grasped his butt cheeks, pressing him closer.

FREE Merchandise is 'in the Cards' for you!

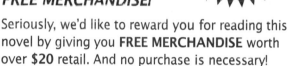

Dear Reader,

We're giving away FREE MERCHANDISE!

Seriously, we'd like to reward you for reading this novel by giving you **FREE MERCHANDISE** worth over $20 retail. And no purchase is necessary!

You see the Jack of Hearts sticker above? Paste that sticker In the box on the Free Merchandise Voucher inside. Return the Voucher today… and we'll send you Free Merchandise!

Thanks again for reading one of our novels—and enjoy your Free Merchandise with our compliments!

Pam Powers

Pam Powers

P.S. Look inside to see what Free Merchandise is **"in the cards"** for you!

W

e'd like to send you two free books like the one you are enjoying now. Your two books have a combined cover price of over $10 retail, but they are yours to keep absolutely FREE! We'll even send you 2 wonderful surprise gifts. You can't lose!

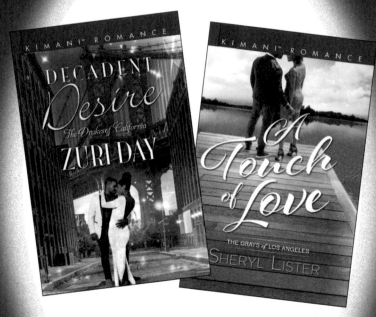

REMEMBER: Your Free Merchandise, consisting of **2 Free Books** and **2 Free Gifts**, is worth over $20 retail! No purchase is necessary, so please send for your Free Merchandise today.

Get TWO FREE GIFTS!
We'll also send you 2 wonderful FREE GIFTS (worth about $10 retail), in addition to your 2 Free books!

Visit us at:
www.ReaderService.com

Books received may not be as shown.

YOUR FREE MERCHANDISE INCLUDES...
2 FREE Books **AND** 2 FREE Mystery Gifts

FREE MERCHANDISE VOUCHER

2 FREE BOOKS and **2 FREE GIFTS**

Please send my Free Merchandise, consisting of
2 Free Books and **2 Free Mystery Gifts**.
I understand that I am under no obligation to buy
anything, as explained on the back of this card.

168/368 XDL GMWC

Please Print

FIRST NAME

LAST NAME

ADDRESS

APT.#   CITY

STATE/PROV.   ZIP/POSTAL CODE

NO PURCHASE NECESSARY!

K-N17-FFM17

The move ratcheted up the level of passion inside him, and she could sense he was rallying to the challenge.

A low, husky laugh escaped his lips. And he began moving faster inside her, demanding she keep up the rhythm he was setting. He was in charge, his hands cupping her bottom as he surged in and out of her again with deliberate strokes. All thought of who was in control left Tahlia's mind. She could only feel the heat of his body, the heavy rasp of his breathing, the slapping of their bellies as he drove harder inside her. She wrapped her legs around his middle, sweeping her fingers down his back.

And when rapture finally hit her, she screamed, and he shouted a purely animalistic cry as their control broke and they came tumbling back down to earth.

Chapter 9

Bare-chested and wearing only his pajama bottoms, Maximus stared out at the Los Angeles skyline. He was bowled over by the lovemaking Tahlia and he shared last night. They'd transcended any other experience he'd ever had. He'd never felt so close, so in tune to another human being. Tahlia had fulfilled every one of his fantasies, and then some. She was so open and honest with her feelings and how much she enjoyed everything he'd done—they'd done. Maximus smiled because he had the scratches on his back to prove it.

And she'd been insatiable for him. They hadn't stopped at one time. They'd made love several times through the wee hours of the morning. He'd particularly enjoyed Tahlia on top as she'd straddled him, easing up and down his shaft. He'd encouraged her, holding her hips to find a rhythm. She'd ridden him until he'd flipped her over and taken her from behind. Images of them together throughout the night flooded his mind.

Maximus wasn't sure he could continue with his seduction scheme. He'd known it was wrong from the start to use another person. But more important, he liked Tahlia a lot, much more than he'd ever imagined he would. He liked her openness, her kindness and her giving spirit. She was a truly unique person, and he considered himself lucky to have met her.

Tahlia emerged from his bedroom sleepy-eyed and wearing the tuxedo shirt he'd carelessly thrown on the floor in his haste to be with her. She looked sexy as hell with her hair mussed and lips swollen and wearing his shirt.

"Good morning, beautiful." He held out his arms to her, but she shook her head and walked toward the overnight bag in the foyer that the driver had to have brought up last night.

"Let me brush my teeth first," she said. She grasped her bag and quickly headed back to his bedroom.

He smiled. He loved the air of innocence about Tahlia. It was appealing given the sophisticated women he'd been with in the past. They wouldn't have dared walk out of his bedroom without their hair in order and face fully made up. Tahlia, on the other hand, looked appropriately bedded. She was down-to-earth, and that was what he liked.

She reemerged five minutes later, and this time her hair had been brushed until it gleamed, and when she came toward him, she smelled clean and minty, like toothpaste and peppermint mouthwash. "Good morning." She kissed him full on the mouth.

He stroked her hair, and she glanced up at him with her big brown eyes, and Maximus's heart turned over in his chest. He couldn't describe the feeling that came over him, only that he didn't want to let her go. He patted his pajama bottoms, making sure he'd thrown in a condom. Then he hauled her closer to him and kissed her again.

She parted her lips and let him devour her mouth. He deepened the kiss, cupping her bottom against his erection because as soon as he'd seen her, he'd come to life. Maximus began walking Tahlia backward toward the couch. They fell on it a mass of limbs, but Maximus recovered long enough to start unbuttoning the shirt she wore. When her breasts were bare to him, he caught one in his mouth and teased it a little with his tongue and then moved to the other one.

Tahlia began writhing on the couch as he trailed hot kisses down her body. He was happy to find she hadn't put on any panties, and he wasted no time easing her thighs apart and burying his face in her womanhood. He dipped his head to taste her, and Tahlia cried out. "Ah…"

He knew how to please her, and she gave herself over to him as he slipped her legs over his shoulders and opened herself up to him. She trusted him now and closed her eyes, allowing him to bring her through the storm as he toyed with her clitoris. She cried out wildly as she rode the wave, allowing him enough time to push down his bottoms, put on a condom and slide inside her as little aftershocks tore through her. He loved how her body clenched around him and would do so again with him inside her.

"Please, Max, please…" She gripped at his shoulders, desperate for him to move.

He took her hands in his and lifted them over her head, then he fixed her with a penetrating gaze. She stared at him for several long moments as she took in the intense look on his face. Then he surged forward— thrusting in and out.

She gasped, working her hips underneath him in tandem with him, and his hold loosened and she laced her fingers with his. Their eyes remained locked as they moved as one flesh. Maximus couldn't break the gaze. As the intensity grew between them, she didn't look away, either. Instead he sank deeper and deeper until finally their bodies shook and her name passed from his lips again and again.

"Tahlia. Tahlia."

After running home to change, Tahlia made it over to her mother's for Sunday dinner with her sister, Kaitlynn. She'd stayed most of the day at Maximus's penthouse, laughing, talking and, of course, making love. The pleasure and satisfaction she'd found in his arms was immeasurable, and she could attest to it thanks to the soreness between her thighs.

Maximus was not only a skilled lover, but a voracious one. She'd never been made love to with such authority and intensity. It was as if he *owned* her body and she'd been powerless to do anything but be as honest as she could be and hide nothing from him. She'd shown him exactly how much she'd desired him when he'd asked if he was pleasing her or if she wanted more of whatever delicious activity they were engaged in at that moment.

She was in so deep with Maximus. She was falling for him, and it terrified her. The emotions she felt for him were much stronger than what she'd felt for Paul.

"Tahlia," her mother, Sophia, greeted her in the hall after Tahlia used her key to come inside.

"Hey, Mama," Tahlia said. Then she sniffed with her nose. "What are you cooking?"

Her mother shrugged. "Just your favorite homemade chicken potpie."

Tahlia smiled. "You spoil me."

"But she made my favorite dessert," Kaitlynn said, rising from the sofa in the living room where she was watching television.

"Hey, sis." Tahlia gave her sister a one-armed hug.

"I like spoiling both my girls," Sophia replied. Then she inclined her head to the bottle of wine in Tahlia's hand. "You want to open that up while the potpie finishes? Shouldn't be much longer now."

"Sure thing." They all filed into her mother's small kitchen, which had only enough room for a four-seater table.

Tahlia looked around. "Mama, we need to get you a bigger place."

"Why?" her mother asked as she fished a wine opener out of one of the drawers and began opening the bottle. "This is just fine for me. No need in spending money just because you have some."

"I know, but you've been here since we were little," Tahlia replied. "You deserve something nicer. Doesn't she, Kaitlynn?" She turned to her sister for confirmation.

"I agree with Tahlia, Mom. You could do better than this place."

"Why would I want to leave?" She pulled three wine-glasses from above her head in the cabinet, poured the wine and handed both of them a glass. "This place has all my memories of you girls growing up." She went over to the doorway and lightly touched the markings that held their growth spurts through the years.

"I know," Tahlia said, sipping her wine. "I just want the best for you."

"And now that you're dating a wealthy boyfriend, it's probably hard to come back down to earth, huh?" Kaitlynn teased, eyeing her.

Tahlia glared at her. "Don't hate just because Max and I are in a relationship."

Kaitlynn's brow rose. "So you're admitting he's your boyfriend?"

"He called me his girlfriend the other day when he introduced me. So yes, I guess I am."

A smile formed on her sister's lips. "Then I'm glad to see I was wrong. The only reason I'd cautioned you to be careful around him was because I thought Maximus was using you for your vote."

"Her vote?" her mother inquired.

"Don't forget, Mama, Tahlia is the deciding vote at Knight Shipping if Maximus and his brother should butt heads."

Tahlia was silent. She hadn't yet been put to the test on what Max's expectation of her was where her vote was concerned. They'd never really discussed it. Did he see it as a foregone conclusion that she would automatically side with him?

"Can we not talk about business?" Tahlia inquired. She was so happy after spending last night in Maximus's arms that she wanted to bask in the moment. "And just have dinner?"

"Of course, sweetheart," her mother said, and Kaitlynn agreed, but Tahlia couldn't quite dismiss her sister's concerns. Maximus knew she was fair and honest. He wouldn't expect her to always agree with him. Would he?

"Good game," Maximus said after he and Griffin finished up their racquetball game at the country club and were now seated at the bar having an afternoon drink. "I am back in my stride now."

"Yeah, yeah," Griffin said, swigging a beer. "Don't gloat just because you won."

"You need to accept the natural order of things," Maximus said.

"Next week, I'll wipe the floor with that smug smile of yours."

"We'll see." Maximus chuckled. "And how is life at the firm?" Griffin was working long hours to become partner at his law firm.

"The usual, eighty-hour workweeks," Griffin replied.

"And is there any woman on the horizon?" Maximus inquired. "Are you holding out on me? I've told you about Tahlia."

"Only as much as you want me to know," Griffin responded. "Besides, there's no one special in my life. Unlike you, who's all Machiavellian."

"That's not true. I care for Tahlia," Maximus replied. "Actually, I like her a lot."

Griffin regarded him quizzically for a moment and then he said, "You're starting to fall for her, aren't you? Now it won't be so easy to go through with this ridiculous scheme you've concocted."

"I admit I've developed strong feelings for Tahlia."

"But have you told her why you started seeing her to begin with?"

Maximus frowned. "Of course not. That would hurt her." And he didn't want that. Tahlia was so sweet. Knowing that he'd been planning on using her to get his way would devastate her.

"Then you're in quite the predicament, my friend," Griffin replied. "Because mark my words, there will come a time when this scheme of yours and your developing relationship with Tahlia will all come to a head. And when it does, it won't be pretty."

Maximus looked at his friend. Was Griffin right? Was he walking into the eye of the storm? Should he retreat and let Tahlia go before either of them got hurt?

Tahlia glanced down at the canvas in front of her. She was working on a new piece that would go with her exhibit. The idea had come to her after the amazing weekend she'd had with Maximus a few weeks ago. Since then they'd been seeing a great deal of each other and not just on the weekends.

During the week, they would go out for a bite to eat, catch a movie or just stay at her place and watch Netflix. Tahlia took great pleasure in showing him how the other half lived as they shared a bowl of microwave popcorn and vegged out in front of the television. She'd even broached the subject of Knight Shipping when they were curled up together.

"Why are you bringing up work?" He'd pulled away to look at her strangely.

"Because…" She'd trailed off. "I want you to share with me what's going on in your world. I may not understand it all, but you could explain it to me. For instance, how's your work on the expansion coming?"

Initially, Maximus had been startled by her request, but eventually he'd started talking about his dream for expanding the company and all the jobs it would bring to the community. He had Tahlia so invested, she couldn't think of a single reason why she wouldn't vote his way.

He'd even introduced her to his friend Griffin, and they'd gone out on a double date with him and a new woman he was seeing. Tahlia had liked Griffin immediately. She could see Griffin could be a ladies' man just like Maximus with his dark chocolate skin, bald head and basketball player build. She also noticed that Griffin was the yin to Maximus's yang. Although he was an attorney, he was much more laid-back than Maximus, but Tahlia was doing her best to change that. She'd even corralled Maximus into going dancing. She was crazy about him, but he was terrible at freestyle dancing, although it didn't matter to Tahlia because she was happiest in his arms.

And the nights, well, Tahlia blushed when she thought about their active sex life. It was a rare night when they didn't make love. Maximus was an imaginative lover, making sure she was satisfied each and every time.

She hadn't realized just how important Maximus had become to her day-to-day routine until he went on an overnight trip during the middle of the week and she was alone in bed and unable to spoon with him. She also hadn't received a phone call from him during the day or a text to see how her day was going as she usually did. And so she had gone up to the gallery loft to paint and while away the hours. She was concentrating so hard on her work that she didn't notice it had become dark or that she had a guest.

Tahlia glanced up and found Maximus staring not just at her, but also at the canvass. "Hey," she said, smiling as he came forward to peer at her artwork.

He brushed the briefest of kisses across her lips and said, "This is good, really good, Tahlia."

She beamed with pride. "You think so?"

"Yes, of course I do. Will this piece go in your exhibit?"

She nodded. "When did you get back?" she asked over her shoulder as she walked over to the sink and washed her hands.

"A little while ago," he answered, still looking intently at her painting. "I came straight here. I missed you."

Tahlia turned around, and the lusty look on Maximus's face made her rush into his arms, wet hands and all. He flattened her against him, branding her lips with urgent, moist kisses, letting her know that he was as desperate as she was to be together.

She stilled. "The door…"

"Faith was leaving when I arrived. She locked up," Maximus said, planting kisses on her ear and neck. "We're alone."

Tahlia quickly began pulling at his overcoat, sliding it down his muscular arms. Then they were both tearing at each other's clothes until they were nude. She didn't think it was possible to get aroused this fast, but Maximus brought out this side to her, made her wanton and greedy.

"I want to see all of you," Maximus groaned as they slid to the floor on top of the sheet she'd used to ensure paint didn't get on the floor. But in this moment Tahlia could care less. She wanted Max. He climbed on top of her, covering her body with his. She opened her legs to cushion his hardness, but he withdrew from her.

"Hold on a second. Need a condom…" he groaned. He reached for the wallet in his trousers to sheath himself and returned to her. When he returned to her, he stared down at her as if he were seeing her for the first time.

She held out her arms, and he sank down, pressing his lips to hers. Then they were once again kissing, tasting and nibbling at each other's flesh. Tahlia's eyes glazed with passion when she felt his fingers at her entrance, sliding deep inside her, making sure she was stimulated, lubricated and ready for him. She whimpered, seeking more of him, and he delivered by removing his fingers, flexing his hips and plunging inside her.

Tahlia arched off the floor, going blind with unimaginable pleasure. "You feel...so good...inside me," she panted as her arousal heightened. "More... Max..."

Maximus wanted to drown in Tahlia and her rising passion. Her core was throbbing tightly around him, milking every last thread of control he had to make this last. So he thrust in again, stroking deeper, and her cries rose and she bunched her hands in his hair.

He withdrew, then plunged in again, burying himself to the hilt. Tahlia shattered around him, but he didn't stop. He couldn't. He was enraptured, and he surged into her again, reaching new heights, so much so that Tahlia's entire body began convulsing around him and his own orgasm tore through him, so hard that he roared out his release so loud he was sure everyone on the street had to have heard him. He fell forward on top of her, then carefully rose on his shins to look down at her.

Her eyes were slumberous, and her entire body relaxed beneath him as aftershocks continued to jolt through their bodies. Maximus didn't disengage from her. He was still hard and throbbing inside her. He wanted her again.

But not here.

They'd go back to her place or his. He didn't care, but he would spend all night making love to her until they both slept.

Later, when they made it back to her place and were cuddled in bed, Maximus knew he wanted to spend more time with Tahlia. He'd known it when he'd lain in his hotel room the night before and missed Tahlia's warm body beside him. He hadn't even stopped at the office, which was his usual MO after a business trip, and headed directly to her gallery. He'd known he'd find Tahlia there, and he had.

She was painting again. And he hoped in part that it was due to his encouragement that hers was as good as any other artist's work that she exhibited at the gallery.

"You awake?" he whispered in her ear when her backside was firmly planted in his crotch.

"Hmm..." she moaned sleepily.

"I was thinking we should go away this weekend, to Big Sur. There's a great place I know of with the best views."

Tahlia turned around in his arms to face him. "You want to go away together?"

He grinned down at her. "Yes, my dear, but only if you don't have any other plans."

"I was going to paint," Tahlia said, stifling a yawn, "but I can finish the piece when I get back."

He grinned. He'd thoroughly worn her out. "I don't want to stop your muse."

She laughed huskily. "You won't. Maybe you're my muse." Her voice was still thick with sleep.

He peered at her intently and wondered if she really meant that or she was just saying it in the heat of the moment. He stroked her cheek. "Go back to sleep, my love, and we'll talk details in the morning." He kissed her forehead and then held her until she fell asleep.

But he didn't go to sleep right away. In his wildest dreams, he couldn't have created a woman who fit him so perfectly. The result was electric, and her unguarded response to him stirred his soul. This furnace of mutual passion couldn't last forever, could it? Surely, they'd blaze out control, but somewhere deep in the recesses of his mind, Maximus wasn't sure that was true—and that scared him to death.

Chapter 10

My love. He'd called her his love. Tahlia could still hear his words as she packed for their Big Sur trip on Friday. She was probably putting too much emphasis on them, but surely they meant something. Or maybe she'd misheard. She had been drifting off to sleep when he broached the subject of a weekend getaway. And he hadn't repeated the endearment since. Not over the phone to say he was working late or again today when he'd asked if she was all packed for the trip.

Tahlia was certainly starting to feel the sentiment, but she was afraid to say it first. With Paul, she'd been quick to reveal her feelings, and look where that had gotten her. Looking at it logically, they'd only been seeing each other a month. So she would keep her feelings to herself until she was sure they were returned and it wouldn't blow up in her face.

She continued packing, putting in warm clothes as well as a swimsuit because Maximus had indicated the room they'd be staying in had a hot tub. Tahlia's face flamed when she thought about what they could do inside that tub. She was so deep in thought that she nearly missed hearing her cell phone ring. When she did, she found it was Maximus's assistant, Elena, calling to inform her of a board meeting next week.

"Will you be attending?" Elena inquired.

Tahlia hadn't given much thought to the running of Knight Shipping because she'd been so caught up with Maximus, taking over the gallery and preparing for her own exhibit. She supposed Maximus had made her and Lucius's life easy by handling the day-to-day operations, but now it was time for Tahlia to fulfill the duty Arthur had given her.

"Ms. Armstrong, are you there?" Elena asked after her prolonged silence.

"Yes, I'll be there," Tahlia replied swiftly. She ended the call and sat down on her bed. When they returned from their weekend getaway, their relationship would be tested for the first time. Tahlia's stomach lurched at the prospect. She could only hope that the foundation they'd made wouldn't crack under the pressure.

Maximus was excited to pick up Tahlia and take her to the Post Ranch Inn in Big Sur. It was known for its romantic rooms with a view, and he'd made sure to select the top-of-the-line room for them. Nestled on a cliff, the room was by far their best, in his opinion. He just hoped Tahlia would like his choice.

She was waiting for him on the sidewalk when he pulled to the curb to pick her up. He jumped out of the car and greeted her with a searing kiss. Then he stepped backward to drink in the cute outfit she was wearing, her usual fashion of skinny jeans and oversize sweater. Tahlia made it look like a fashion statement. She'd put her hair up in a chignon with loose tendrils framing her face and wore minimal makeup with the exception of lip gloss.

"Let's go," Maximus said, opening the passenger door for her. "I want to get on the road before traffic picks up."

"Of course." Tahlia slid inside while he dealt with her overnight bag.

The drive to Big Sur was uneventful, and they chatted conversationally about the week. But Maximus noticed that Tahlia didn't bring up the fact that Knight Shipping had a board meeting coming up when they returned next week. He'd forgotten it himself until Elena had reminded him this morning and begun contacting board members, including Lucius.

His brother had been sure to tell Elena that he wouldn't miss it. Maximus had no idea how the meeting would go. He suspected that Lucius would be as ornery as possible just to get under his skin as he had on the tour, but it was Tahlia he was most concerned about.

Maximus just wanted it over with as quickly as possible. He'd been running the company the last month quite well without either Lucius's or Tahlia's assistance or interference. Thankfully, they'd taken a back seat and let him do the job he'd been groomed for.

He looked over at Tahlia. She was staring out at the coast, and he wished he could be as carefree as she was in this moment. He would try his best not to think about next week and be in the moment with her. She must have sensed him watching because she glanced over at him and smiled. Maximus's heart swelled in his chest.

They arrived to the inn in a little under three hours and walked a short cobblestone path to the cliff room. When he opened the door, he let Tahlia precede him so he could see her enjoyment.

* * *

Tahlia glanced around and was shocked at just how stupendous the room was after they'd entered it from an enclosed garden courtyard. It was a freestanding structure and held a massive king-size bed. And directly in front of her was the breathtaking view through the glass-walled bedroom. She glanced at the wood-burning fireplace on her way to the deck. Once outside, she could see they were suspended on a cliff. They could watch the sunset and sit on the two loungers outside or in the stainless steel outdoor hot tub.

Tahlia turned to Maximus, who'd followed her. "You've outdone yourself, Max."

He smiled. "I'm glad you like it."

"What's not to like? This is every woman's romantic getaway."

"C'mon." He grasped her hand. "You didn't see the rest."

He led her back into the living area and past the bathroom's glass door so she could see the soaking tub. "How would you like a bath in that?"

She grinned mischievously as she pulled him closer. "Where do I sign up?"

They spent the rest of the afternoon touring the inn's amenities before retiring to their room to change for dinner. They both dressed casually, Maximus in slacks and a button-down shirt while Tahlia opted for knit slacks, an oversize sweater and some flat sandals. Being in the mountains, it was a bit colder than in Los Angeles, but Maximus told her he'd keep her warm. Tahlia had no doubt he would; it didn't take much to stoke the flames of their desire for one another.

The dinner at the inn's restaurant, Sierra Mar, overlooked the coast and offered a stunning view. Tahlia felt like she hadn't been living fully until she'd seen nature in all its splendor. After dessert, they retired to the room, where Maximus made gentle, sweet love to her, touching her in places that made her quiver and moan in pleasure. She called out his name more than once because he satisfied her every need. Eventually, they both drifted off into a peaceful sleep.

Maximus awoke on Saturday morning feeling better than he ever had. He felt rejuvenated even though he'd gotten very little sleep. He'd thought he had an insatiable appetite, but Tahlia more than matched him in sexual compatibility. The way she'd stroked him with her searching fingers, he'd been unable to resist her, and he'd succumbed willingly to her.

And now, as he drove them to the Esalen Institute, Tahlia talked animatedly about the institute and all of its offerings. When he'd thought of Big Sur, the nonprofit retreat center had come to mind because Tahlia always seemed so self-aware that he thought she'd appreciate its emphasis on the mind-body connection. Plus, there were tons of workshops on self-help, gardening and Tahlia's favorite: art. Max suspected they'd spend their entire Saturday there. He wondered if the weekend could get any better. Why had he never taken the time to get out and smell the roses? Because he'd always been trying to please his father. A wasted effort.

Tahlia's first activity choice was for them to take a meditation class. Maximus hadn't been interested, but Tahlia had talked him into it. He didn't see the purpose of sitting for an hour and focusing on his breathing, but afterward he had to admit he felt more relaxed and less stressed than he had in a decade.

"See? I told you you'd like it," Tahlia said as they

left the yoga studio and began to explore the farm and the institute's sustainability program before venturing to the art center.

Maximus knew that Tahlia would appreciate the painting workshop, so he left her there and took in a leadership workshop. He immersed himself for an hour in the transformation leadership session about how he could live his authentic self while nourishing the lives of others.

They ended their self-reflective day with hour-long massages followed by a dip in the hot springs. He and Tahlia opted to wear swim trunks and bathing suits while others went with the clothing-optional route. Maximus thought Tahlia would shy away from the experience, but then she'd surprised him by removing her bikini top and then her bottom and luxuriating in the water.

"Don't be afraid," she teased as she stood there completely nude.

Her abandon caused Maximus to lose his trunks and circle his arms around her. They basked in their freedom until the sun began to set and it was time to head back to the inn.

It was by far the most liberating experience Maximus had ever had. Tahlia brought out a different side of him, a more playful side. Instead of following a set, rigid path, she was opening him up to new experiences and allowing him to let go. He wasn't sure he'd fully be able to thank her for the joy she was bringing into his life. All he could do was show her.

After showering, they donned the thick terry cloth robes that came with the suite and chose to have room service outside on the deck facing the cliffs. Tahlia stepped outside first, giving Maximus just enough time to slide a condom into his robe pocket. When he joined her on the deck, the staff had already set up a candlelit table for two with silver domes covering their meal.

"I really enjoyed today," he said, staring at her from across the table after they were seated.

"Which part?" she asked, amused. "Your meditation workshop? No, wait, I bet it was that leadership talk. That had to be really gripping." She chuckled to herself.

"You know that wasn't it."

"Oh, no?" she asked, her eyes filled with glee.

"It was seeing you take off your bikini and bask in your nudity."

A blush crept up Tahlia's face, starting from her neck and moving to her cheeks. She looked downward and then up at him. "I've never done that before."

"Gone skinny-dipping?" He'd done it only once, at Harvard as part of a dare.

She nodded. "No, not ever. I was living in the moment."

"So am I." Maximus rose from his chair, and in two steps he had Tahlia in his arms. He would have loved to have made love to her in the hot springs, but they were not alone, so he'd had to temper his passion for her, but not now. He wanted her hot, naked and bucking underneath him. He reached between them and untied the knot, letting the robe slip from her shoulders and fall to the floor. Then he grasped both sides of her face and kissed her like he'd wanted to do earlier.

Tahlia wrapped her arms around Maximus's middle as he made love to her mouth. His tongue darting in and out was such sweet torture that she moaned. She arced her body to find contact with him, eager to relieve the friction between her thighs, but instead of giving her what he wanted, his lips left hers, sliding down her body to the swell of her breast. She was so sensitive that when he drew the first bud into his hot waiting mouth and laved it with his tongue, she moaned. When she swayed, Maximus kept a steady hold on her, keeping her upright. Then his mouth traveled slowly down her breasts to her belly until he was bending before her and cupping her swollen mound.

"Oh, yes," Tahlia moaned when he slid a finger inside her folds.

"Does that feel good?" He glanced up at her; his eyes were molten fire.

"Y-yes," she cried out softly, not sure she could survive the pleasure Maximus was inflicting on her most sensitive place.

"How about that?" he asked, adding yet another finger inside her and swirling it around.

"Oh, God, yes…" Tahlia threw her head back in abandon.

"Then you're going to love this." He replaced his fingers with his mouth, and she closed her eyes, leaning her head against the glass doors of the deck as he took her to ecstasy.

Maximus thought he would dictate the pace of the evening, but he'd been wrong. Tahlia was a force to be reckoned with, and she was showing him that she wanted him to possess her. He quickly pulled out a condom and barely had time to put it on before Tahlia threw her arms around his neck and wrapped her legs around his waist. Maximus knew what she wanted and what his body demanded, and he thrust upward, sinking into her with an animalistic shout.

"You're mine, Tahlia," he groaned when she began

moving her hips deliberately, letting him know that he was hers, too.

All he could do was stand firm, supporting her weight with his hands clasped under her buttocks as she ground her hips up and down on his shaft, driving them both to the peak of ecstasy and back again. He could feel her inner walls contracting all around him, and this time, Maximus was the first to cry out his release, with Tahlia following an instant later as she bucked against him.

Limp, her legs fell to the floor, so he moved swiftly, lifting her in his arms and carrying her to the bed. Then he lay down beside her, amazed at how perfectly they fit together. He'd never let go like that with a woman. He'd always been sure his lovers came first, but he'd been powerless to resist Tahlia's hold over him.

They'd come together like two forces of nature, but now he wanted to take his time and slow the pace of their lovemaking. They continued kissing, touching and teasing until they both fell into an exhausted yet blissful sleep.

Chapter 11

"I'm in love with Maximus," Tahlia told Kaitlynn after returning from her Big Sur getaway the next day. Her sister had stopped by the gallery to preview some of the selections Tahlia might put up for her exhibit. The words just slipped from her lips because she'd been dying to say them out loud and had almost said as much in Big Sur when Maximus had made love to her so gently, her eyes had filled with tears. But she'd kept the words to herself. Tahlia wasn't sure how Maximus would react or what he would say. She knew he was into her—that much was obvious. But how much? Did it transcend the physical like it had for her?

"Wow! Okay." Kaitlynn sat across from Tahlia in her office and leaned back in her chair. "I certainly wasn't expecting that revelation today. Do you feel better now that you've said it out loud?"

Tahlia nodded.

"Has Maximus said the words back? Has he told you he loves you, too?"

Tahlia shook her head. "No, because I've only told you."

"Me?" Kaitlynn's voice rose an octave. "I would think you'd be telling him. You know, shouting it from the rooftops and all that. You're the romantic one, while I'm the practical one."

"Well, I'm being practical here," Tahlia responded ruefully. "I'm not sure of Maximus's feelings for me—" she drew her brows together "—or at least not entirely, so I'm kind of playing it close to the vest."

"Because of Paul?"

"You know how open I was with him. How I just laid my heart bare only to find out we weren't compatible. I won't do that again, Kaitlynn. I have learned from my past mistakes."

"Of course you have. But don't you think you should try to see how Max does feel about you?"

Tahlia came from around her desk and sat beside Kaitlynn. "Yes, I do…"

"But…"

"I don't know, something's holding me back."

Kaitlynn stared at her. "You don't trust him entirely, do you?"

Tahlia bowed her head. She didn't want to admit that Kaitlynn's warnings had merit. Tahlia didn't really know what Maximus expected from their working relationship, and because of it, despite how much she'd fallen for him, she hesitated revealing her true feelings for him.

"Tahlia?"

When she finally glanced up, tears shone on her lashes. "I worry that you could be right about Max."

"That he could be using you for your vote?"

Tahlia nodded. "I don't want to have these doubts, Kaitlynn, and he's never asked me to vote for him, but at the same time I can't ignore that they're there and they're valid. We did get involved so quickly. Yet we've never really talked how my two percent share and vote would work, but I guess I'll find out soon."

"What's going to happen to help you decide?"

"We have a board meeting at Knight Shipping. It's the first one since Arthur's death. Both Lucius's and my attendance is recommended. I know I'll be there, and I'm sure Lucius will be, too. It amuses him to toy with Max."

"So you'll find out Maximus's true motives then," Kaitlynn said. "Surely that must give you some comfort that you'll know one way or another how he truly feels about you."

"Does it?" Tahlia inquired. "Or will it shatter all my hopes and dreams of a future with Max?"

"You could talk to him now before the meeting. See where his head is. And if he's honest with you, you'll know where you stand."

Tahlia nodded, but she was scared to face the truth. She didn't want to lose what she had with Maximus, but if they didn't have honesty and trust, the foundations of any good relationship, what did they have?

"Maximus." His mother beamed when he stopped to visit her at the estate on Tuesday evening. He hadn't seen her much in the last few weeks because he'd been spending much of his time with Tahlia or staying at his own place. Even though he'd spent the entire weekend with Tahlia at Big Sur, he'd still stayed at her place the last two evenings since their return.

"Mother." He kissed both of her cheeks.

"Where have you been hiding yourself? I've barely seen you."

"I've been staying at the penthouse."

"During my time of need?" she queried.

Guilt assailed Maximus. She was right. His father had been gone only a couple of months and she was still grieving, although in his opinion, Arthur Knight did not deserve her tears, or any emotion, for that part. Since the truth about Lucius had come out that night at the hospital, Maximus had found it hard to have any sort of compassion for him.

However, he'd been a good son and stood by his father's bedside as he'd tried to recover from the massive heart attack he'd had while in bed with Jocelyn, but that was as far as it went. It was as if the love he'd once had for his father had evaporated. Not that Maximus had shown his love easily. Why should he when Arthur had always rebuffed his overtures?

Maximus could remember a time when he was nine years old and he'd been so proud of a project showing the creation of Knight Shipping and all that his father had achieved. His father had scoffed at it and asked him if that was the best he could do. Maximus had immediately smashed the project until it lay in tiny pieces on the floor.

"Max, are you all right?" his mother asked when she noticed he was a million miles away, in the past with all the memories of a father who'd never truly loved him.

He blinked several times. "Yes, I'm fine. And I'm sorry I've stayed away too long. Come, let's have dinner together."

He stayed at the estate with his mother and shared their cook's delicious dinner, but Maximus felt uneasy. He usually enjoyed his mother's company, but not tonight. There was a nagging in the pit of his stomach that he just couldn't shake, and he moved the food on his plate from one side to the other.

"You don't like the squab?" his mother inquired, peering at his full plate.

He glanced down at the tiny fowl and shook his head. "It's fine. I mean, it's delicious."

"There's something on your mind. What is it, Max?"

Maximus glanced up at her. "Hmm…"

"It's the board meeting tomorrow, isn't it?"

His brow furrowed. "How did you know about that?"

"Just because I'm not involved in Knight Shipping doesn't mean I don't know what's going on. And it's your first meeting since your father died."

"True."

"And it's the first time that you'll find out just how bad you'll butt heads with your father's illegitimate spawn."

"Mother, must you call him that? He is my brother, after all."

"A brother you never knew anything about."

"And whose fault is that? All the adults in our lives made sure Lucius and I could never get to know each other. Maybe if we had we wouldn't be at each other's throats now." Maximus pushed back from the table and began pacing the floor. "This could have all been avoided if you, Father and Jocelyn, for that matter, had been honest."

Charlotte Knight rose from her seat in a flurry. "I'll tell you what it would have been like, Maximus. Your father would have left us to be with his other family, leaving me to raise you alone. That's what would have happened. I did what I had to do to keep my family intact, to make sure *my son* was on top."

Maximus sighed heavily. "And in the end it was all for naught, wasn't it? Because I'm not on top, Mother, and I never will be. I have to share the throne with Lucius."

His mother's head dropped down, and tears slid down her cheeks. "I'm sorry, Max. If I had any idea that your father would have done this, I would have…"

"Blackmailed him into keeping me as head of Knight Shipping?" Maximus snorted. "All that would have brought about is more hate and animosity from him, and I think I got plenty of that when he was alive."

His mother held her head in her hands and began sobbing. Maximus rushed over to her and pulled her into his arms. He held her until her sobs began to quiet. "I'm so sorry," she murmured against his chest. "I did my best."

"I know you did," Maximus responded softly. He couldn't be mad at her. She was the only family he had left. Or was she? He did have a half brother, but there was no way a relationship between the two of them was possible.

"And tomorrow—" she glanced up at him "—do you think the Armstrong girl will vote your way now that you've been seeing each other?"

Now there was a million-dollar question if ever there was one. He'd set out on a path to seduce Tahlia, and in the end it was he who'd been seduced by her, by her beauty and by her spirit. But tomorrow was judgment day. He'd shared with Tahlia his feelings about expanding Knight Shipping. She knew how much it meant to him. But he also couldn't ask her to vote with him. He wanted her to do it because she believed in him. But would she? Would Tahlia vote with him or against him?

Tahlia was uneasy as she prepared for bed. She'd been antsy all night, and even a cup of her favorite chamomile tea had done little to help calm her frayed nerves. She was on edge about tomorrow's board meeting. She knew the significance of the meeting and the possibility of brother-against-brother, and it weighed heavily on her mind. After leaving Kaitlynn, she'd thought she'd feel better. She'd spoken her feelings aloud. But she hadn't told the one person who mattered most: Maximus.

If theirs was a normal relationship, she might be willing to take the risk, but it wasn't. There was a thread linking the two of them together. A thread that threatened to destroy everything between them.

Tahlia was surprised when her doorbell rang. It was after 10:00 p.m., and she was getting ready for bed. She had on her favorite nightie and bunny slippers, and her hair was tied in an unattractive messy bun. She peeked through the peephole, and her breath caught in throat. Maximus was standing on the other side. What was he doing here so late?

He knocked softly on her door. "Tahlia?"

She didn't hesitate and swung open the door. He was leaning against it, looking sexy in jeans and a pullover V-neck sweater. "Max?"

He walked toward her, pulled her in his arms and kicked the door shut with his foot. Then he began kissing her with such masterful passion that she lost her breath. She reacted without question and curled her arms around his neck and kissed him back. Then she jumped into his arms, wrapping her legs around him. He caught her and carried her to the bedroom.

They didn't talk as they undressed each other. Instead, Tahlia merely lifted her arms so Maximus could remove her nightie as she kicked off her slippers. And he did the same when she pulled his sweater off and reached for the zipper on his jeans. She pushed them and his briefs down his legs, and he stepped out of them; his perfect body was completely open to her gaze. They met on the bed, falling back against the pillows. He tugged the clip in her hair free and glided his fingers through her tresses.

It felt good to have him touch her. And when he dipped his head to kiss her and she felt the stubble on his cheek, Tahlia was happy he'd come. They could have this one last night together before circumstances inevitably forced them to make a stand. When she felt his tongue darting through her parted lips, she went mad, kissing him back with everything she had. There was nothing more arousing, except maybe having him inside her.

She sighed with delight when Maximus left her lips and began to tongue her ear and nip at her neck. As he moved away and went lower, Tahlia shamelessly thrust her breasts at him, and he took the bait. He toyed with them first, playing with her nipples between his thumb and forefinger, and then his mouth was on her, laving her with hot flicks of his tongue.

When he finally suckled them, Tahlia bucked as the sensations he evoked ricocheted through her. But he didn't stop tormenting her. His path went downward to her belly. He teased her with light kisses and soft touches. His hands caressed the curve of her hip and thighs, but instead of going to the place she wanted him to, he flicked his tongue across the sensitive spot at the back of her knees and went lower to massage her calves and feet.

"Max…" He knew where she wanted him and the heat of his mouth. But he was deliberately drawing out the pleasure.

He glanced up at her. His eyes were heavy lidded with desire as he kissed his way back up her legs and thighs, stroked her belly, then paused, hovering over the place that ached for his touch, his fingers, his mouth. "You want me here?" he teased.

She nodded enthusiastically.

When he bent his head, she weaved her fingers through his curls and waited, waited for him to make her his, because she was. At the first flick of his tongue on her, Tahlia ground her hips into the bed as fire raced through her veins at the contact. Her every nerve ending was on fire waiting for his next action. Maximus teased the nub at the center of her with gentle flicks, stimulating her sensitive tissues, and when he darted his tongue inside her, Tahlia became unglued. She cried and keened as his clever tongue and fingers drew out a scream and her first orgasm surged through her.

Maximus lapped up all of Tahlia's sweet nectar but didn't stop tormenting her. After he'd left his mother at the estate, he hadn't known where he was driving until he'd ended up at Tahlia's doorstep. Tomorrow would bring their first real test, and he was afraid of what might happen. As much as he wanted to ask Tahlia to vote with him, he didn't. He needed to know if she'd do it on her own because she cared for him and wanted what was best for *him*.

Maybe deep down he knew the answer and that tonight might be potentially the last time he would ever have her. If so, he was going to make it count. He cupped her buttocks and thrust his tongue deeper inside her. Tahlia panted uncontrollably as he continued his determined assault. Her second orgasm came quickly, and she yielded every inch of herself to him.

It was only then that Maximus sheathed himself with the condoms he'd kept in his pants pocket since meeting Tahlia and slid up her sweat-slick body. He wanted to be inside her, but Tahlia pushed him backward and climbed on top of him. She took his erection in her hands and traced the length of him. Maximus hissed out a breath when both her hands encompassed his girth and she took him inside her mouth.

He heard a moan escape his lips as he felt her take him deeper into her moist, silky mouth. He reveled in the way her tongue swirled around his length and how she paid special attention to the crown, teasing it with light flicks of her tongue. He threw his head back and accepted her ministrations not only because it felt good but because he was with Tahlia, a woman he'd come to care about greatly and could possibly love.

When he could take no more, he flipped her over onto her back and kissed her. The sigh of pleasure that escaped her lips was cut off by Maximus entering her, possessing her, inhabiting her completely. He pressed his lips into hers and thrust his tongue inside her as the lower half of him did the same. Her answer was to roll her hips to give him better access. And so he moved deeper, and Tahlia accepted him greedily, hungrily, bucking and writhing underneath him.

That was what he loved about her, her openness, her lack of inhibition when it came to their lovemaking. She let him know that she enjoyed every minute of it. So he thrust into her more steadily, bringing both of them to the precipice, then easing back. He would make the moment last. He raised himself on his forearms and slowly thrust in and out of her. Tahlia splayed her hands across his chest and then upward to encircle his neck, urging him to pick up the pace.

He compiled and pounded into her over and over again. She gasped but clung to him as he built up their pleasure until finally the world turned on its axis and everything dissolved and pure bliss coursed through them.

Maximus fell on top of Tahlia, and she accepted his weight, holding him to her. When their breathing returned to normal, he slowly released her and lay back against the pillows. Tahlia curled up beside him, her head on his chest. It felt so natural to be with her that he drifted off to sleep.

Chapter 12

Maximus stood at the head of the table in the Knight Shipping conference room at the Wednesday meeting. He'd left Tahlia's in the early-morning hours to get back home and face the day. He hadn't wanted to disturb her. No, that was a lie. He was afraid to face her and see doubt or confusion in those brown depths, so he'd taken the easy way out and slipped out of bed while she was sleeping.

Now he watched the executive leaders and heads of departments enter the room. He'd asked them to attend so he could introduce them. The board meeting was being held in the next fifteen minutes, and neither Lucius nor Tahlia had arrived yet. It gave Maximus a few minutes to get his head on straight. Most of the meeting was routine and would require very little input from either one of them. However, there was one item on the agenda that required a majority vote.

He wanted to take the company public. Knight Shipping had come a long way, but in order for the company to expand and compete with the big boys, it needed to become global. He'd discussed it with his father before he'd passed, and Arthur had adamantly refused. He'd wanted it to stay a family business, but Maximus had disagreed. It had been a source of contention between them. Maybe that was why Arthur had decided to split his shares of the company with Lucius—to make sure it would never happen.

Maximus was hoping to convince Lucius and Tahlia that it was the right move. Lucius had to realize it was the right move. He'd seen for himself at the shipping yard that they were at capacity. Plus his own company, Knight International, was a publicly traded company, as was his fiancée's, and they'd both been quite successful. He wanted the same for Knight Shipping.

Lucius stepped into the boardroom several moments later. Maximus glanced in his direction. His older brother looked ever the businessman in a sleek gray suit and tie. His hair was neatly cropped as always. Maybe if things had been different they might have had a relationship, but now they were on opposite sides.

When Lucius saw him standing at the far side of the room, he strode toward him. He extended his hand. "Maximus."

Maximus was surprised he wasn't calling him Max again to rile him up. "Lucius." He shook his hand.

Lucius glanced around at all the people in the room. "Are all these people really necessary? Aren't you, Tahlia and I the only shareholders?"

"Yes, but I thought you'd like to meet some of the heads of the departments and see who works for you," Maximus responded smoothly. "Not all of them were on-site during your tour."

"Of course. Good thinking. Where's Tahlia?"

Maximus hated that Lucius was using her first name. He didn't know her like Maximus did, as *intimately* as he did. As if her ears were ringing, Tahlia entered the room just then in a stunning suit that Maximus suspected was new. She didn't usually wear suits. Her style was much more bohemian chic. He watched her long legs as they strolled toward him, and his mind went to the two of them in bed last night and how he'd taken her from behind just that morning.

She smiled at both men when she made it to their group. "Lucius, good to see you again." She held out her hand.

Lucius accepted and patted her hand. "Tahlia. You're looking well. Actually, might I say, glowing?" He glanced in Maximus's direction. "Life is certainly agreeing with you."

Tahlia blushed. "Thank you." She hazarded a glance at his direction. "Maximus."

He noticed that she called him by his given name and not Max, like when they were together. Did that mean something? There was also a question lurking in her eyes, like why hadn't he kissed her goodbye when he'd left?

"Tahlia." Maximus nodded his head and looked down at his watch. "We should get started." He moved away from the duo and toward the head of the table. He cleared his throat. "Good morning, everyone. I'd like to get started. I'm sure you'd all like to get back to work."

There were several laughs and guffaws, but eventually they all took their seats. Lucius flanked Maximus's right while Tahlia opted to sit at his left. When he glanced in her direction as he sat down, she gave him a tentative smile.

"I'll call this board meeting to order," Maximus

stated and looked at his assistant, Elena, to record the time since she was taking the minutes.

The next hour went by quickly, with Maximus reviewing typical business matters and introducing the executive team and key department heads. Lucius asked questions occasionally while Tahlia was silent and wrote notes in a folio she'd brought with her, but Maximus knew it was the calm before the storm.

"Now on to new business," Maximus said. "As many of you know, Knight Shipping has had an excellent last decade, but our reach within the United States and abroad has reached its full potential. In order to go after new contracts, we need to expand, but as good as we're doing financially, we just don't have the working capital for a project of this magnitude."

"I'm in agreement. Expansion is always good," Lucius stated. "I mentioned as much during the tour. But why is this on the table now? I'd thought I'd have time to review your proposal beforehand." He eyed Maximus suspiciously.

"There's a multimillion-dollar deal to transport luxury vehicles that's come across my desk, but the only way we can go after it is if we expand."

"What do you propose we do?"

"We need to go public."

"Pardon me?" Lucius asked in a chilly tone.

Maximus turned to stare at him. "You heard me. If we go public, we can raise the capital we need to expand Knight Shipping and finally reach our full potential."

"But Knight Shipping is a family company, is it not?" Tahlia inquired, finally speaking for the first time.

"Yes, it is," Lucius stated, glaring at Maximus.

"Don't dismiss this out of turn," Maximus replied. "Going public makes sense. Elena, will you hand out the prospectus? This will show what impact transporting the additional goods will have on our bottom line."

His assistant rose from her post at his side to hand out packets to each person at the table. Maximus watched Lucius and Tahlia look over the materials. The room was silent as they both absorbed the material. Maximus knew some of it was over Tahlia's head, but she was bright enough to catch on, and if not he'd explain it to her, make her see how good this could be for the company.

It was Lucius, however, who spoke first. "Looks like you've done your homework, Max."

Maximus bristled. He'd resorted to calling him by his nickname. He took it to mean he'd gotten his older brother's ire, which wasn't a good sign of things to come.

"Yes, I have, and the name's Maximus."

"How long have you been working on this?" Lucius inquired. "You couldn't have come up with all this—" he pointed to the prospectus on the table "—in the last couple of months. So how long?"

"Does that really matter?" Maximus responded.

Lucius spun around in one of the executive chairs. "Yeah, it kind of does. Because if you've been working on this for months, it means you'd have brought it to Arthur's attention, and if you did, this would already be in the works. But since it's not, it leads me to believe that he shot you down."

"Is that true?" Tahlia asked softly from his side.

Maximus glanced at Tahlia. The look she gave him was both inquisitive and suspicious. He knew because he'd seen all of her looks, or at least he thought he had, until now.

She was silent as she waited for him to respond.

"Yes. I had mentioned this to my father."

"You mean *our* father," Lucius asserted.

A horrified gasp echoed from around the table.

"I mean, my father," Maximus repeated determinedly, "but he was too shortsighted to see what going public would do for our company."

Lucius stared at him. "Going public would mean we—" he pointed to both of them "—would have to put up our shares. What exactly is your intention here, Max? To have me put up all my shares and leave me with no stake in the company?"

Maximus snorted. "As I said, I presented this idea to my father well before I knew of your existence."

"But you're presenting it now, why?"

"Because it's an excellent idea."

"I don't think that's why," Lucius responded, folding his arms across his chest. "It's because you want to get rid of me and dilute my shares so that you end up as majority shareholder."

"That's not true," Maximus stated.

"Is he right?" Tahlia inquired, peering at him incredulously. "Is that why you're bringing this up now? I mean, we've hardly had time to process the fact that we're shareholders. And I know how badly you want to expand, but you want us to make this decision now."

"Time is of the essence, and we need to start moving on this."

Silence ensued at the table for several long moments.

"I'm inclined to agree with Arthur. If he didn't want this for his company, why should I go against his wishes?" Lucius inquired.

"You didn't even know him," Maximus stated vehemently.

"Through no fault of my own," Lucius returned

evenly. "And I'm not going to get into that right now. So my vote is no."

"You haven't even given this due consideration," Maximus replied. "This is a good deal. It will create hundreds of jobs and make Knight Shipping a force to be reckoned with. If this were one of your other companies, you wouldn't hesitate to pull the trigger. You're voting no out of spite just to see me fail."

"You have no idea how I feel," Lucius said. "And perhaps in time I'll change my mind, but at this moment the answer is no. And since your vote is undoubtedly yes, that leaves you, Tahlia." He looked at her from across the table. "Where do you stand?"

Maximus wanted to know the same thing and looked at Tahlia. His eyes pleaded with hers to trust him, to believe in him that he knew what was right for Knight Shipping and that he'd never lead them astray.

Tahlia glanced at Lucius and then at Maximus. He could see she was torn. This was a big decision. No, it was a monumental one. Because not only was she voting about whether to take Knight Shipping public, she would also be voting *for* or *against* Maximus. One outcome would mean they could continue on and flourish in their relationship knowing they were of one mind. The other outcome, the more treacherous one, possibly meant the end of a good thing. A good thing Maximus didn't want to let go, but ultimately it was Tahlia's decision. Same as it had been when they'd become involved.

"My vote is no," Tahlia finally said quietly.

"What was that?" Lucius asked. "Because I don't think everyone heard you. For the record, please, if you could speak up."

Tahlia looked at Maximus as she spoke. "My vote is no."

Maximus felt his heart closing in on itself, but he refused to allow his outward appearance to belie his inner turmoil and that his heart was breaking. "All right, let the record state that the vote is two to one and with fifty-one percent of the voting shares. This issue of going public is tabled. I believe that concludes new business, unless anyone else has anything else to add?"

As he looked around the table, he could see the disbelieving looks of his executive team, who knew going public was a solid move. "Then the Knight Shipping board meeting is concluded. Thank you, everyone, for attending."

Maximus closed the folder on the table that contained all the work he'd been diligently working on over the last year to convince his father and now Lucius and Tahlia to vote his way. But he'd failed once again. He rose to his feet and headed for the exit.

"Maximus, wait!" Tahlia caught up with him at the double doors. "Can we talk?"

"Not now, Tahlia," he said firmly, his mouth a grim line. "Not now."

Tahlia stared at Maximus's retreating figure and moved aside as the other meeting attendees left the conference room. She could feel tears stinging her eyelids, but she had to keep it together. She couldn't cry in front of them.

"Are you all right?" Lucius asked from her side.

Tahlia shook her head and felt him softly grasp her arm and pull her inside the now-empty room. Before she knew what was happening, he'd pulled her into his embrace, and she finally let out the tears she'd been holding in.

"There, there," he calmed her as if she were a small child as she cried into his no-doubt designer suit.

When she finally lifted her head, Lucius was looking down at her. "Come, sit." He guided her to a nearby chair, and once she'd sat, he offered her a handkerchief from the inner pocket of his suit jacket.

"Thank you." Tahlia sniffed, accepted the hanky and began blowing her nose. Why did she have to break down in front of Lucius of all people?

"He'll get over this," Lucius stated.

She glanced up at him. "Who?"

He smiled knowingly. "My brother."

"I don't know what you mean."

"No need to be coy, Tahlia. I know you and he are involved," he responded.

Her brow furrowed. "How?" Was she really that transparent?

He shrugged. "It's not hard to figure out after your reaction to him leaving just now. But to be frank, I noticed Maximus's interest in you from day one when we were at the estate and again during the tour. And from what I've heard, it's only progressed since then."

"Have you been having us followed?" She was horrified at the prospect.

Lucius shrugged. "Suffice it to say, I've been keeping an eye out on my baby brother. And I can see how much he's come to care for you and vice versa."

"You can?"

Lucius grinned, and Tahlia could see why Naomi had fallen for him. When he wasn't annoying Maximus, he was quite attractive. Of course, she had eyes only for Maximus, who now was so angry with her he didn't even want to talk to her, much less look at her.

"I can because I know it's how I felt when I fell for

Naomi. My grandmother said it was written all over my face, and I can see what she means because it's written all over yours."

Tahlia attempted a laugh. "It won't do much good now. Maximus hates me."

"He doesn't hate you. He may be angry with you. He may even feel a bit betrayed by you since you sided with me about going public, but he doesn't hate you."

Why hadn't she thought through her vote? She'd cursorily glanced over the expansion prospectus without giving it due consideration. She'd been so focused on honoring Arthur's wishes and projecting her own opinions and views about the man who'd been a father figure to her that she'd neglected to take into account Maximus's feelings. "What do you suppose I do?" Tahlia inquired.

"Ah." Lucius leaned back in his chair. "That's where you have me at a loss. I wish I knew my brother better to offer you some sound advice, but I don't. I only know how I would feel in this instance, and I would say to give him some time to settle down and let cooler heads prevail."

"Why are you telling me all this?" Tahlia inquired. "I'd think you'd want him to be unhappy."

He frowned. "Why would you think that?"

"Because," Tahlia responded, "you don't miss a chance to antagonize him. Get his goat. You know you do."

Lucius grinned mischievously. "I suppose I do sometimes, but isn't that what big brothers are supposed to do? Give their little brothers a hard time?"

Tahlia stared at Lucius for long moments, and then it hit her. "You want a relationship with Max, don't you?"

Lucius's mouth compressed and he was silent, and

Tahlia wondered if he was going to answer her, and then he said, "Yes, I do. I grew up an only child, Tahlia, and I've always wanted siblings, and now I have one but he doesn't want me." His eyes drifted to the closed door beyond which Maximus was down the hall in his office, probably seething with fury at what he considered her betrayal.

"I think he wants it, too," Tahlia said. "He's just afraid to admit it." She knew she was revealing a confidence, but maybe there was a way she could finally bridge the gap between these two proud and powerful men. So she continued. "Just because Arthur acknowledged him doesn't mean Maximus had it easy growing up, Lucius. Arthur was cold and distant with Maximus. Constantly pushing him to excel but never showing him affection. And in the end, giving you, us—" she pointed back and forth between them "—half the company he'd worked so hard for. He has a right to his anger. But I also know he doesn't blame you about your parentage. In fact, he's been angry with both your mothers and father for how they all handled the situation. You both could have known each other, grown up together, been a family if they'd all let go of their individual agendas."

"I couldn't agree with you more," Lucius said. "About our parents, that is. And thank you for sharing with me about Maximus's childhood. Being acknowledged as Arthur Knight's son wasn't all it was cracked up to be. I'd always thought the grass was greener on the other side. Clearly, I was wrong."

"I need to go to him." Tahlia rose to her feet. She couldn't just wait and see what happened between them. She had to know now, make him see that her vote today had nothing to do with her feelings for him or what he meant to her.

"Tahlia." Lucius touched her arm. "I know how much you want this, want my brother, but be careful. He's angry right now and he might lash out."

She nodded. "I understand." But she had to act. If she waited for the dust to settle, it might only push them further apart. She had to trust her instincts. He may not be ready to say he loved her, but deep down she knew Maximus would never hurt her.

Chapter 13

Maximus returned to his office after his epic fail of a board meeting and found Griffin waiting in his office. He frowned. "What are you doing here, Griff?" He tossed the folder with his proposals on the desk. He might as well burn it for what good it had done him today. He'd known Lucius would vote against him, but he'd been hoping against hope that he was wrong about Tahlia and that she'd pull through for him. For once, he needed someone to be on his side. But yet again, he'd been wrong. Why did everything have to be so hard?

"I thought you might need to see a friendly face," Griffin said. "When you texted me yesterday that today was the big vote, I wasn't sure how it would go for you."

"Well, it didn't." Maximus stalked to his desk. He reached inside his drawer and pulled out the bottle of bourbon he kept for special occasions to toast a good deal with the executives. But today was different. He *needed* it to take the edge off. He produced two small glasses. "Care to join me?"

"If it'll make you feel any better, then sure, I'll have

one." Griffin regarded him from the sofa, where he was perched.

Maximus poured two generous glasses and then walked over to hand one to Griffin. "Bottoms up." He didn't wait for Griffin and instead chugged the amber liquid back in one gulp.

"Take it easy, Max," Griffin said. "I know things didn't go your way today, but that doesn't mean it's over."

"Doesn't it?" Max's brown eyes stared at him. "It's over, Griffin. I'm tired of beating my head against a post and going nowhere. Maybe Lucius—" he pointed to the door, glass still in hand "—and Tahlia should see what it's like when there's no one at the helm. Let's see how they fare without me. I'm going on an extended vacation."

"To punish them for voting against you?" Griffin inquired. "Won't this hurt you in the process? You're a major shareholder, too, Max. Think about what you're saying."

"I don't care," Maximus replied, walking over to the bottle of bourbon and pouring himself another glass. He gulped down the second drink. "Damn my father for putting me in this position."

"There's nothing you could have done."

"Clearly, I didn't do a good job seducing Tahlia," Maximus said bitterly. "I should have never gotten involved with her when she was just a means to an unfruitful end. Our entire relationship was a complete and utter waste of time."

"Don't say that, Maximus, because I know that's not true." Griffin put down his glass and stood. "I've seen how you've changed since you've been with Tahlia.

You're more relaxed and carefree. Lighter even. She's been a good influence on you."

"I don't want to talk to her right now."

"Why not? Why can't you say how you feel about her?" Griffin inquired.

"Because she betrayed me today," Maximus hissed through clenched teeth. "She could have been on my side, but instead she sided with him."

"Your brother."

"My enemy."

"I don't believe that's how you truly feel. We've always been like brothers and you've always wanted a sibling. Well, you have one now. Maybe if you opened your heart, like you've done with Tahlia, and let love in. Then maybe…"

"Love has n-e-v-e-r done anything for me," Maximus responded bitterly, cutting him off. "Anyone I've ever loved has either lied to me, thrown it back in my face or betrayed me. I can do without that emotion, thank you very much."

"Fine. Then wallow in self-pity, Maximus, but I have to say the look of poor little rich boy doesn't look good on you."

Seconds later, he was gone, leaving Maximus alone. And this time, he truly felt that way.

Tahlia hid behind a planter as Griffin stormed out of Maximus's office. She'd heard more than she'd ever wanted to. And now her heart was breaking just like Maximus's. She caught sight of him sitting on the floor with his drink just as the door closed.

Tahlia swallowed the bile in her throat, and with as much decorum as she could muster after hearing that Maximus had purposely set out to seduce her, she made her way through the front doors of Knight Shipping and out to her car.

She sat inside for minutes, hours—she truly couldn't count because all she could do was hear Maximus's words reverberating through her mind. *I should have never gotten involved with her... Our entire relationship was a complete and utter waste of time.*

She was in stunned disbelief. He truly felt like getting involved with her was a complete and utter waste of time? Sobs took over her, bubbling over, and she cried until there were no more tears left. She knew people had to wonder why she was still sitting in visitor parking, but she physically was unable to move until the sobs subsided.

Eventually, Tahlia drove herself home. On the way, she called Kaitlynn, who promised to be there waiting for her. And she was. As soon as she opened the doors to her apartment, Kaitlynn was there, enveloping her in the warmest of embraces.

"Thank you, Kaitlynn." Tahlia clung to her baby sister as she closed the door behind her. Kaitlynn led her to the sofa, and Tahlia curled into a ball in the corner. She felt like such a fool for believing that Maximus had ever meant one word he'd ever said to her. *She was just a means to an unfruitful end.* Maximus's harsh words still stung hours after she'd heard them.

"Tahlia, what happened?" Kaitlynn asked. "You were kind of incoherent on the drive home, and I couldn't make out what you were saying."

That led to another round of fresh tears, and Kaitlynn stopped talking and merely held Tahlia as she let out the grief. "It was all a lie, Kaitlynn," she finally was able to say. "He was using me."

"No!" Her sister didn't want it to be true, and neither did she. She'd believed Maximus, *in him*, that he would never hurt her, that somewhere deep inside him, despite the trauma of losing his father and experiencing his indifference that he was someone capable of genuine feeling, but she was wrong. Maximus Xavier Knight was a cold, heartless bastard who cared about no one but himself.

"It's true," Tahlia responded. "He hoped that by seducing me, I'd be more pliable and would vote his way." She laughed, and her laughter turned to tears. "Of course, he got the shock of his life today when I voted against him, despite the fact that he'd made sure I fell for him. And I did, I fell hard for a liar. Are all the Knight men untrustworthy?"

Tahlia thought of Arthur and the years he'd lied to Charlotte and Jocelyn, to his sons, to himself. Maybe Maximus just didn't know any better. Look at his role model.

"I don't know what to say, Tahlia," Kaitlynn said. "I was rooting for Maximus. I was hoping that my sixth sense was wrong and that he was on the up-and-up. I'm sorry I was wrong and that I didn't do more to dissuade you from going down this path."

"Like you could have stopped me. I wanted Maximus from the moment I first saw him, and when he opened the door for a possible relationship, I walked right through it. Knowingly and happily."

"That still doesn't mean it doesn't hurt."

"Nope. It hurts like hell. It feels as if I'm literally being torn asunder." Tahlia held her stomach, which had been tied in knots since the board meeting. It had only worsened after she'd overheard Maximus's angry words.

"What are you going to do now?"

"At this very second?" Tahlia asked. "I'm going to

stay on my couch until the pain hurts a little less. And then tomorrow, I'm going to go into the gallery and run my business."

After Paul, she'd sat on the couch in her pajamas eating pizza and ice cream and in general feeling sorry for herself, but not anymore. She'd become stronger after him and knew that eventually the hurt of losing Maximus would ache a little less.

Kaitlynn smiled at her. "I'm proud of you, sis. If this had been Paul, you would never leave this house."

"Oh, I want to curl up in a ball and die," Tahlia said. At Kaitlynn's shocked look, she clarified, "Not literally, that is. But as much as I love Maximus, I can't change what's happened. Somehow I'll have to find a way to go on without him."

Maximus's head was pounding and his mouth tasted vile. He glanced around and realized he was at his penthouse and had fallen asleep on his sofa wearing yesterday's suit. The last clear memory he had was of being in his office yesterday with Griffin and having a bourbon. The room was spinning, so he laid his head back down, and that was when he recalled that his assistant, Elena, had called him a cab when she'd found him passed out in his office. He must have stumbled up to his penthouse on his own. Thank God he hadn't driven.

He sucked in a deep breath. Drinking hadn't changed the situation, it had only given him a hangover. Maximus vowed not to do that again. He was still in the minority at Knight Shipping, a company he'd always thought would be his someday. And now that he was no longer angry, he felt defeated. His father had set all of this in motion, but that still didn't mean that he wasn't hurt that Tahlia didn't believe in him, wouldn't stand by his side. She knew how he felt about Lucius, about the entire situation, and still she'd voted against him.

The more he thought about it, the angrier Maximus got. He needed to talk to Tahlia, if only to clear the air so he'd have no regrets. Gingerly, he eased himself off the sofa and headed for the shower.

Fifteen minutes later, he felt refreshed from the hot water and was dressed and ready to face the day. He thought about calling Elena or checking his email, but he'd been serious yesterday when he'd told Griffin he was taking a break from Knight Shipping. He'd let Lucius and Tahlia run the business in his absence. Instead, he spent the remainder of the afternoon making arrangements to take out his father's sailboat. Maximus had always loved the boat, and that was the one thing Arthur hadn't managed to give away during the reading of the will.

Once he had a captain lined up and arranged for provisions to be delivered to the sailboat for that evening, he packed a large suitcase because he wasn't coming back. At least not for a while. But before he could head to the marina, he needed to have a chat with a certain lady.

He took the Bugatti and arrived at Tahlia's apartment after 7:00 p.m. But he wasn't prepared for the reaction that greeted him. As soon as Tahlia opened the door and saw it was him, she slammed the door in his face.

Tahlia couldn't believe Maximus's nerve. He'd actually shown up on her doorstep after all the hideous things he'd told his best friend. What did he want? One for the road? A quick roll in the hay for old times' sake? She didn't want to let him in, but his incessant knocking and calling out her name was causing a disturbance to her neighbors.

She swung open the door but hung on to it. "What do you want, Maximus?"

His eyes widened at the use of his full name, but he didn't say anything. Instead he just stood there staring at her. "Can I come in?"

"Why?"

"Because we need to talk."

"We have nothing to say to each other. I heard quite enough yesterday."

His brows drew together in confusion. "I don't know what you're talking about."

"Does 'I should have never have gotten involved with her when she was just a means to an unfruitful end,' or, 'Our entire relationship was a complete and utter waste of time' ring a bell?" Tahlia inquired, her arms folded across her bosom.

His face clouded with uneasiness, and his dark eyes shuttered. "Tahlia."

He stepped forward, but she held out her hand as a defense mechanism. "Oh, no, you don't." She shook her head. "I'm not letting you in. So, what, you can sweet-talk your way out of this? I'm not that gullible, Maximus. You may have fooled me once, but not again. I won't be made a fool of for a second time."

"It's not like that," he replied. "You heard that conversation out of context."

She frowned. "By all means, explain."

"Not out here," he whispered when one of her neighbors passed by. "Let me in."

She glared at him and widened the door so he could enter, but she remained rooted to the spot. She wasn't getting comfortable. She would never be that way with him again, and that broke her heart after everything they'd been to each other. They'd been together only a short amount of time and it may not have meant anything to him, but it had meant everything to her.

"I'm sorry you heard what you did," Maximus said, turning to face her at the door. He stood rigidly in the middle of the living room as if afraid to come near her.

"No, I heard the truth, the unvarnished truth. And I'm thankful for it because now I know everyone was right when they warned me to stay away from you. My sister, hell, even Lucius, warned me to be careful, but I wouldn't listen. I had stars in my eyes where you were concerned." She shook her head in dismay. "What a fool I was."

"You're not a fool, Tahlia," Maximus replied. "Our relationship was real."

"*Was*, as in the past tense? So you admit it's over?"

"It's what you want, isn't it?" he inquired. "Because I don't see how we can go on. You're angry with me because of what you heard, and I get that. You have every right to be. I did intend to seduce you, Tahlia, to use you for my own gain, but somewhere along the line that changed and I abandoned that plan because I came to care for you. Truly care for you. But yesterday, you hurt me, too."

"What? You're going to put this on me?" Tahlia stared back at him in amazement.

"You knew how much I needed you on my side," Maximus stated. "How hard it's been for me growing up without my father's support. All I've ever wanted was for that man to believe in me. And in the end, he still didn't because he left Knight Shipping to not only Lucius, but you, too. He didn't even trust Lucius and me to figure out things on our own. He put you in the middle."

"That's not my fault."

"No, it's not, but you put yourself in the middle yesterday," he stated. "You asked me to share my world with you, and I did. I told you about how my father treated me with disdain, never showing me an ounce of the love or affection he so clearly felt for you. I shared my dreams for Knight Shipping and how much I wanted to expand, and yet you still didn't vote with me. And you didn't even have to vote against me. You could have abstained, but you didn't. You didn't support me, Tahlia. Instead, you shot an arrow straight through my heart by siding with Lucius, my enemy. You didn't even have the decency to read all of my proposal before you shot it down."

There was truth to Maximus's words. It was like he was shining a mirror on her faults, too, when she'd always thought she was on high moral ground. "I suppose you're right. I've failed Arthur and you. But Lucius doesn't have to be your enemy, Maximus."

But he wasn't hearing Tahlia. "He is, and because of him you've succeeded in mortally wounding me. I have nothing left to fight for. So you and Lucius can have the company. I'm done with it!"

"How dare you!" Tahlia shouted, rushing at him. "How dare you put this all on me! I admit I'm not perfect and I may have been on my high horse where Arthur was concerned, but *you* set out to seduce *me*! I didn't come after you. I only wanted to fulfill Arthur's wishes and see that you and Lucius got along."

"And I was wrong," Maximus admitted. "Am wrong," he corrected himself. "I shouldn't have mixed business and personal. And I take responsibility for my actions, and I'm truly sorry about that." He started toward the door.

Tahlia peered at him. "And that's it? That's all you have to say to me?"

"What more do you want from me, Tahlia?" Maximus asked.

I want you to love me, Tahlia thought. *Say you love me now and it might make it all better.* Then she could say those three little words back. She could admit she wasn't entirely blameless when it came to what went wrong between them. But he was silently staring at her, or should she say through her, as if she wasn't there. He'd checked out, checked out on her.

"There's nothing I want from you, Maximus. You can see yourself out." She spun on her heel and raced from the room.

When Tahlia made it to her bed, she threw herself down and clutched her pillow. Then Tahlia heard the click of the door as Maximus departed from her life forever.

Chapter 14

Maximus was enjoying his new carefree lifestyle. There was something to be said about letting go of all the entrapments that held him down and just being one with the sea. He'd been on the sailboat for two months and was enjoying the simple life.

He'd spoken to Griffin and his mother a handful of times, if only to assure them that he was all right. Otherwise, he kept his phone off. Occasionally, he'd turn on it and there'd be voice mails, texts and emails from Knight Shipping, which he'd promptly delete. It was time he started living life for himself instead of doing what was expected of him. It certain hadn't gotten him anywhere except with half a company and a broken heart.

Thanks to having so much time on his hand, Maximus had come to realize that he'd fallen in love with Tahlia Armstrong. He didn't know when it'd happened or how because he certainly hadn't been looking for it. It had just sneaked up on him. The knowledge didn't make him feel warm and fuzzy.

It felt bittersweet because their relationship had been

doomed from the start. Not just because he'd begun seeing her with the intention of seducing her, but because she held the key to something he'd desperately wanted but would never obtain. His father's love. His father's respect. Instead, all he'd ever gotten was his scorn. And a whole lot of confusion because if his father had never inserted that clause, Maximus might never have met Tahlia. And his life had been the richer for it, if only for a little while.

And so, he'd tuck his love for Tahlia away with the love he'd once felt for his father and had never had returned. Love had never been kind to him, so why should he freely give it again? Maybe if he stayed on the sailboat long enough he would finally forget about her.

Hell, he doubted it.

At night, Tahlia haunted his dreams. Deeper and sweeter than if she was with him in person. The smell of her perfume, the way she moaned when he was inside her or the giddiness she had when she'd just finished one of her paintings. He couldn't escape the images of her in his mind, so he stayed at sea hoping to rid himself of the memories. Memories he wondered would ever die.

"Your exhibit, baby girl, is everything," Sophia said as she and Kaitlynn admired Tahlia's art on display one Tuesday evening. Her collection was a mix of oil paintings, charcoal freehand artwork and several ceramic pieces.

"I'm with Mama on this one," Kaitlynn said. "You've truly outdone yourself, sis. I knew you were talented, but this is remarkable."

Tahlia beamed. "Thank you, guys." It was wonderful to receive praise from her family, but there was one person whose praise she desired most. Maximus. True to his word, she hadn't heard from him since he'd quietly left her apartment two months ago.

As the weeks had gone by, she'd begun to realize how incredibly unfair she'd been to Maximus. Forcing her view of Arthur on him and holding Maximus to an unreasonable standard, given all his father had put him through. Tahlia wanted to tell him that she'd *heard* him. No, that she *understood* his feelings and his disappointments about his father, his brother and even their relationship. Sure, she was mad as hell that he'd set out to seduce her, but she hadn't been an unwilling participant. She'd been crazy about Maximus from the moment she'd laid eyes on him. Her hope was that maybe one day they could wipe the slate clean and start again.

But he'd disappeared and left Los Angeles entirely. No one had seen or heard from him or knew how to locate him. They only knew that he'd chartered his father's sailboat and taken off for parts unknown. He'd left Knight Shipping without a word, forcing both Lucius and Tahlia to step in and handle day-to-day operations. Tahlia was learning more than she'd ever cared to learn about the shipping industry.

She'd much rather be here at the gallery in her element or painting, but being a shareholder in the business forced her to care about its goings-on. Robert Kellogg and the executive team were helpful, but she and Lucius were learning to lean on each other and becoming friends in the process. He wasn't half-bad, and Tahlia only hoped that one day Maximus would be able to see that, see that he could have a relationship with his older brother if he wanted one. Lucius was certainly open to it.

Despite all the upheaval, Tahlia was happy that her work was finally on display. She'd worked hard over the last few weeks finishing up the pieces. Everyone who was anyone in the Los Angeles art community and neighboring cities had been invited to the event. She was hoping for some positive press, which would encourage her to continue painting. Not that she'd ever stop. Painting was catharsis for her and was helping heal the wound that losing Maximus had cost her.

"Would you like some champagne?" she asked her mother when the waiter came around with a tray.

"Absolutely," Kaitlynn answered for her and reached for three glasses. She handed each of them a flute. "We have to toast the lady of the hour." Kaitlynn raised her flute. "To Tahlia—we hope all your dreams come true."

They clinked glasses and each took a sip of champagne. "Thank you, sis."

Faith rushed over to Tahlia. "Come, that indie magazine I told you about is here and would like a quote from you for their arts section."

"Excuse me for a second." Tahlia went with Faith to answer the journalist's questions.

Three hours later, the gallery was empty, and she and Faith were left to clean up after the caterers she'd hired for the event had left.

"Everything okay, boss?" Faith asked when she noticed Tahlia was introspective. "I would think you'd be smiling given the fantastic turnout we had and that half your pieces were purchased."

"I am very happy," Tahlia said, feigning a smile as she began turning off lights throughout the gallery.

"Why do I hear a *but* in there somewhere?"

Tahlia shrugged. "I don't know. Something's just missing is all."

"You wouldn't mean a curly-haired shipping magnate, would you?" Faith raised a brow.

"Am I that obvious?"

"Only to someone who's worked with you for three years," Faith responded. "I've never seen you as happy as you were when you were seeing Maximus. I hate that you've broken up. Do you think there's any chance you'd ever get back together?"

"That's doubtful, Faith," Tahlia responded when they'd finally made it to the front door.

"Just thought I'd ask." Faith squeezed her shoulder. "Stay strong, okay?"

"I will." But it was hard to do because deep down, although she wouldn't admit it to her family, Tahlia missed Maximus and wanted him back. But as long as she was a shareholder in Knight Shipping that would never happen. Tahlia took one final look at the gallery and then locked the door.

The seas were choppy. Maximus wished the sailboat was closer to dry land, but they were at least an hour out from the Los Angeles marina. After two and a half months at sea, he'd finally decided to come home, if for nothing else than to see his mother. She'd sounded lonely the last time he'd spoken to her, and Maximus had realized how selfish he was being by staying away when she had only him. So he was coming home. At least for a short visit.

He would stay for a couple of days during the week and be back on board by the weekend, but the weather was bad. Had been for hours. After putting on rain-coats, he and the captain had battened down the hatches and were now waiting out the inclement weather inside the galley kitchen with some black coffee with a hint of bourbon.

"You sure you're ready to come home?" Roy inquired

when he glanced at Maximus. He'd shared some of what happened with the will, Tahlia and Knight Shipping with the captain. The older man hadn't offered any advice. He'd just listened to Maximus ramble on about losing his company and his woman. "I thought you were adamant about staying away."

"I was."

"What changed?" Roy inquired.

"My mother. She's missing me, and I kind of took off unexpectedly. I didn't even see her before I left, so I'm coming back for a quick visit."

"And then going back out again?"

"Probably."

"Just let me know. I'm at your disposal."

"No one you want to go home to?" Maximus inquired, raising a brow.

"Not at the moment, sir."

Maximus nodded. It was the opposite for him. He had his mother. And, of course, there was Tahlia. When he'd docked in Marina Del Ray, he'd caught sight of a Los Angeles newspaper and seen that she'd finally had her art exhibit. They were touting her as the next great artist. He was proud of Tahlia and that he'd encouraged her in some small way to achieve her dreams, even if he wasn't there to see it.

Just then, a loud knocking hit the portholes of the galley. "Maybe one of the sails came loose," Roy commented. "I'll go on out and take care of it."

Maximus shook his head. The man was nearly seventy years old, and even though he could more than handle himself on the sailboat, it would be easier for Maximus to maneuver. "You stay. I've got it."

Once he was outside, the rain beat down on Maximus, soaking him right through the raincoat he had on.

He was starboard when the one of the booms lurched at him. He tried to duck, but it was too late, and seconds later he was knocked unconscious.

"Tahlia, it's Lucius," a deep masculine voice said from the other end of the line early the next morning.

"Lucius, what is it?" Tahlia said as she rubbed sleep from her eyes. She glanced at her clock on her nightstand. It read 5:00 a.m. Her buzzer hadn't yet woken her to get up. "You sound funny. Is everything okay?"

"It's Max."

Tahlia's heart lurched as foreboding shot through her, and she sat straight up in the bed. "What's happened to him?"

"He's been injured in a boating accident and is en route to Cedars-Sinai Medical Center. I just thought you might want to know."

"I do. Thank you so much, Lucius. I'm on my way." Then she paused. "Are—are you going?"

"Yes, of course," he stated. "He's my brother."

The phone line went dead, and Tahlia rushed around her bedroom to find something to wear. As she threw on a pair of yoga pants and a T-shirt, Tahlia didn't know what to think. Lucius hadn't said much. She just prayed that Maximus was okay and that his injuries weren't serious.

When she arrived at the hospital twenty minutes later due to light morning traffic, Maximus's mother, Charlotte, Lucius and Naomi were already there.

Tahlia rushed forward. She glanced at Charlotte, but she looked so distraught as she sniffed into a Kleenex that Tahlia didn't dare speak to her. She went to Lucius, and he reached for her, grasping her hands in his. Lucius looked equally desolate and not put together like he usually was. He and Naomi both wore track suits.

"How is he?"

Lucius shook his head. "We don't know yet. They just brought him and are assessing his injuries."

"What—what happened?" Tahlia could barely get the words out as images of Maximus bleeding on the floor of the sailboat assailed her.

"He was knocked over by one of the sails and hit his head," Lucius replied. "We don't know much more than that."

Tahlia nodded. "How's his mother?" She inclined her head toward Charlotte Knight, who was sitting with Maximus's friend Griffin.

"A wreck," Naomi answered her this time. "I thought she wouldn't appreciate Lucius and my being here, but when she saw us she almost seemed happy that she wasn't going to go through this alone. I think she's frightened of losing Maximus, too, after losing her husband."

"That's understandable," Tahlia said. Her heart went out to Charlotte even though his mother had been less than kind to her previously. "I'm going to go sit with her."

And that was where Tahlia remained for hours because the ER doctor had come out to inform them that Maximus needed to go into surgery to repair the brain bleed from the injury he'd sustained on the sailboat. At the news, Charlotte had begun weeping uncontrollably, and it had taken both Tahlia and Naomi to calm her down while Griffin and Lucius remained stalwart. Eventually, Charlotte and Naomi dozed off. Unfortunately, Griffin had to depart because he was due in court, but he promised to be back. So Tahlia stood to stretch her legs and to check on Lucius.

She found him outside the ER staring ahead of him—at what, Tahlia didn't know.

"Hey," she said, coming to stand beside him.

He looked down at her, and the despair she saw in his dark eyes startled her. Tahlia had known Lucius cared for Maximus, but she hadn't known just how much until now. Tahlia reached for his large hand and squeezed it.

"He's going to pull through this, Lucius. He has to."

Lucius glanced upward at the sky. "I don't pray, Tahlia. I never have, but I have been now. I can't lose…" His voice caught in his throat. "I can't lose my brother, too, not when I've never really gotten to know him."

Tahlia nodded as tears filled her eyes. "And you won't. *We* won't. He's healthy and strong. He'll pull through. You'll see."

Lucius sucked in a deep breath. "Thanks, Tahlia. Where's Naomi?"

"Dozing with Charlotte."

He nodded. "All right, we'll let them rest."

"While they're resting, why don't we head to the chapel?" Tahlia suggested. She wanted Maximus to have all the prayers they could both give. Knowing that she could lose Maximus and seeing how short life was had Tahlia reevaluating her feelings. When he woke up, maybe it was time to tell him just how much she'd missed him and that she loved him.

Maximus had a splitting headache. This was nothing like the hangover he'd had after he'd lost the vote at Knight Shipping months ago. This was much worse. Except this time, when he opened his eyes, he wasn't in his room or on the sailboat, which was the last place he remembered being. He was in a hospital room.

He blinked several times, trying to remember how he'd gotten here, but he couldn't. He could see, however, that someone's head was lying on the hospital bed beside him. He reached out and stroked the person's hair, and instantly the smell came to him.

Tahlia.

At his touch, she lifted her head and looked at him sleepily. Her brown eyes connected with his dark ones.

"Max?" she whispered. And then she blinked several times, as if she wanted to make sure she wasn't dreaming and that he was real.

"Yeah, I think that's my name," he said groggily with a half smile. His head felt foggy. Was he medicated?

"I'm so glad you're awake." She rose to her feet. "I have to tell your mother and Lucius." But before she could move away, he caught her arm.

"Wait. What are you doing here? What am I doing here? What happened?" He launched several questions at her.

She paused midstep. "You were in an accident on your sailboat on your way back to LA. You suffered a brain bleed and they had to go in and operate."

"So that's why my head feels so fuzzy?"

She nodded. "You've been out for almost twenty-four hours."

He glanced at the door. "Mother?"

"Lucius was able to get her to sleep in one of the empty rooms. Nearly browbeat every administrator he could for the privilege. I'll go get her." She started to move again, but once again, he stopped her.

"Are you coming back?"

Dared he hope?

"Yes."

Maximus watched Tahlia depart. So he wasn't dreaming. She was here and apparently had been at his bedside. For how long? How long would she stay by his side before circumstances inevitably forced her to leave him and he was alone again?

Chapter 15

Once outside the room, Tahlia clutched her hand to her mouth and allowed the sob of relief she'd been holding in to escape her lips. He was awake. Max was going to pull through. Her prayer—heck, all their prayers—had been answered. She'd wanted to jump up and dance, but the wary look Max had given her made her pause. She couldn't tell if he was happy to see her or not. But he had asked her if she was staying. Surely that meant something.

"Tahlia." Lucius strode toward her down the hall. "Is he okay? Is my brother still alive?" The fear in his tone was evident because Tahlia had felt the same fear herself over the last forty-eight hours.

Tahlia glanced up at Lucius. Tears winged her eye-lashes, and she nodded. "Yes, yes." She clutched his muscled forearms. "He's fine. He's awake and asking to see his mother. I was just headed to find Charlotte."

"Oh, thank God." Relief flooded across Lucius's face as he rubbed his hands across his face. Tahlia could see just then what the threat of losing Max had done to Lucius. Worry creased his forehead, and his eyes were haunted. He'd been so strong holding it together for her and Charlotte, belying his own inner turmoil, but she could see now, when he let down his guard, just how scared he'd been.

"It's a miracle," Tahlia said with a smile. "You should go see for yourself." She inclined her head toward the door, but Lucius shook his head.

"No, he wants to see his mother first, not me."

"Lucius…" Tahlia stared back at him incredulously. "You've been at this hospital for two days, same as the rest of us. You have a right to see him."

"Do I?" Lucius asked with a grimace. "I'm not sure Maximus would agree with you. And I don't want to upset him, not now when he's recovering. I'll be around."

Her brows furrowed. "Are you sure?"

Lucius nodded. "It's enough that he's awake and stable. Come, let me take you to Charlotte."

Tahlia allowed him to walk her down the hall, but she glanced back at Maximus's door. What would it take to get the brothers to finally see the truth—that the family and love they'd always wanted was right there in front of them if they would only reach out and grab it?

"It's all right, Mama." Maximus had never called her anything other than Mother, but in that moment, seeing her break down as she sat on the edge of his hospital bed, it felt right. "It's okay." He patted her head as she bowed her head on his chest and wept. "I'm going to be okay."

"I—I—I just thought I was going to lose you," she cried into his chest. Maximus wrapped his arms around her as best he could with all the IV lines and drips around him taped to his hands and arms.

"You didn't," he stated firmly. "I'm here and I'm not going anywhere."

Finally, she lifted her gaze to meet his, and it was like Maximus truly saw her for the first time in years. And as he did, he could see she'd aged nearly overnight. Her usually coiffed black hair was in a ponytail, *a ponytail* of all things. Her eyes were puffy, red-rimmed with circles around them from lack of sleep. And she was wearing jeans with a cardigan sweater set. He'd never seen Charlotte Knight ever look so, so *casual*.

"I'm just thankful I wasn't alone," she said. "Your girlfriend, Tahlia, has been here with me this entire time."

"She's not my girlfriend, Mother. We broke up before I took off when she found out about my plan to seduce her when we first met."

"I beg to differ. That girl has been by your bed this entire time and by my side. She truly cares for you, Maximus. No, it's more than that." She shook her head. "She loves you."

"That may be so, but the circumstances that led to our breakup to begin with are still there, and that hasn't changed."

"Oh, honey." His mother's voice softened. "Are you sure there's no way to salvage your relationship? I admit I initially was angry with Tahlia for the fact that Arthur shared confidences with her that he didn't share with me, but I can't blame her for that. Instead, I've found her to be a warm and caring person, and I'm seeing what Arthur saw in her. She's a great listener. It's as if you can tell her anything without any judgment. It must be how he'd felt."

Maximus turned his head and looked away. "I don't

want to hear about Father now." Because she was right. It's how Tahlia made everyone feel, including him.

"And should I take it you don't want to talk about your brother, Lucius, either?" she asked. "Because he, too, has been at the hospital since he learned of your accident. He hasn't left this place, and he's made sure you've received the best possible care. He even flew in the best brain surgeon in the country to be on your case."

Maximus turned his head. "And where is he now?" he inquired caustically. "Why isn't he in here right now making sure I'm all right?"

His mother shrugged. "Maybe because he doesn't think he'd be welcome, and can you honestly blame him? You haven't exactly rolled out the welcome mat. But then again, neither have I. His very existence is a reminder of the failure of my marriage. Sometimes, it's hard for me to look at him because he reminds me of your father. He even resembles him."

"I can only imagine how hard that must be for you, Mama," Maximus said softly.

"It is." She wiped away an errant tear from her eyes. "But don't you worry about me." She lightly patted his chest. "I just want you to get better. That's what we all want."

"That's right," Tahlia said from behind her. She stood in the doorway carrying two foam cups with what Maximus could only assume was coffee. She walked toward them and handed one to his mother. "Charlotte, I brought this for you. Thought you might need it."

"Thank you, dear." His mother accepted the cup. "I did." She rose from his bed and patted the spot she'd vacated. "You sit and talk with Maximus for a spell. If you don't mind, I'm going to run home for a minute and take a quick shower."

"Of course." Tahlia nodded, smiling at her. "I'll stay here with the patient."

Once she'd gone and it was just the two of them, a silence fell over the room. Instead of sitting on the bed as his mother had done, Tahlia pulled up the chair she'd been sleeping in earlier and scooted it back toward the bed.

"I hope you don't mind the company?" she asked somewhat tentatively.

He shook his head. "No, I'm glad you're here."

"You are?" The hope in her voice was evident.

"I missed you."

She lowered her head as if she was fighting with herself, but eventually she lifted it long enough for him to see tears were shining in her eyes. "I missed you, too."

They both fell back into silence.

Tahlia was the first to speak. "You don't know how scared I was for you," she started. "I thought I might lose you. We all were scared to death. And it wasn't just me, Maximus. It was your mother and Lucius and Naomi."

"I heard he was here."

"He's been here this whole time," Tahlia said. "But that's a fight for another day." She inhaled deeply. "What I'm trying to say is…"

"Is what?"

Her brown eyes were misty and wistful, and Maximus's heart constricted. He wasn't sure he was ready for her next words, but they came all the same. "I love you," she whispered.

She stared at him, waiting for his reaction. Maximus didn't know if it was his brain injury or something else, but he was speechless for the first time in his life. He couldn't think of a single coherent thought. His mind was buzzing from Tahlia's confession.

"The thing is, having you nearly die has shown me life is too short, and I couldn't let another moment pass without telling you how I felt because I might not ever get another chance. I love you," she said it again. "I think I have since I first saw you at the gallery."

Maximus frowned. He didn't remember meeting her at the gallery. They met at the estate when she came for the reading of the will.

At his confused expression, she continued. "You didn't notice me back then. You were there for your father, and after speaking with him, you left shortly thereafter, but I never forgot you. And I suppose when the opportunity came for us to be more—" she paused "—I jumped on it. And I know that you seized on the opportunity to 'seduce' me, but it didn't take much doing"

"Tahlia."

"You don't have to say it back," Tahlia said, patting his hand on the bed. "I understand if you don't feel the same away about me, especially after I put Arthur's feelings and wishes above yours and voted against you. You had thirty years with the man to see his true character. While I only had a year to get to know him. Maybe I only saw what I wanted to see because I needed a male figure in my life and he fit that role."

At her words, Maximus's heart constricted in his chest. "You don't have to say that."

"Yes, I do. Because it's true. I treated you unfairly, and I was wrong. You had a right to your anger. He was your father, not mine. I'm not completely blameless in all this, and I know we were only together for a short time, but I just wanted you to know that—that it impacted me." She bunched her shoulders. "Anyway, I just wanted you to know, and I'll be here until you get better."

Tahlia's love was a gift he didn't deserve. After everything, Maximus didn't feel he deserved her or her love. She was too special of a woman to be with a man like him. Even knowing that he might not say the words back, Tahlia had still put herself out there and told him how she felt. While he sat in his bed, afraid to say the words back even though he felt the same way. He was cold, unfeeling and manipulative, same as his father. She needed someone better than him.

"Thank you," he finally said.

Consternation crossed her face. Had she been expecting him to utter the sentiment back even though she'd said otherwise? Maximus couldn't. He was afraid to. The last time he'd shown someone love, his father, it had been thrown back at him. He feared the same thing happening with Tahlia, and he couldn't bear it if she pushed him away, too. And that couldn't happen, because there was still a hurdle facing them. A hurdle neither of them was talking about.

"Yes, thank you," he said again. "You're amazing, Tahlia."

"But?" The sparkle and light that had been in her eyes a moment ago when she confessed her love had gone out.

"But I'm not sure I'm capable of loving you back," Maximus said finally.

"Capable of loving me? Or you don't at all?" Tahlia inquired.

"Does it really matter?" he said. "There's too much water under the bridge."

"I don't believe that." Tahlia rose to her feet and

peered down at him. Tears were streaming down her tapioca-colored cheeks. "I know we have something, Maximus. Please don't do this. Please don't push me away. Not again. Not after we almost lost you."

"I'm not pushing you away," he said. "You just deserve someone better than me."

"I don't want anyone else," she cried.

"Then you should!" he shouted back at her.

"Max..."

"Maybe you should just leave," Maximus said, turning away from her. "My head is starting to hurt." His heart broke as he heard Tahlia crying behind him, willing him to turn around, but he didn't look back. He couldn't. He was too afraid to take the risk. And so he heard her footsteps as she walked away and most likely out of his life for good this time.

Tahlia was stunned and leaned against the wall of the hospital corridor. She'd never expected Maximus to shun her after she told him she loved him. She slid down the wall into a heap on the floor, and her head fell forward as she sobbed.

She could hear people passing her by, but she didn't care. Embarrassment was the least of her worries. She couldn't move because this time Maximus had hurt her worse than before. This time, she'd put her heart and soul before him on a platter, and he'd just thrown it aside as if her love didn't matter one iota to him.

How could he be so cruel? So heartless?

She was still sitting on the floor when Lucius walked toward her. He crouched in front of her, an angry frown on his features. "What did he do now?" Lucius asked, glancing at the closed door of Maximus's room.

She shook her head.

"Here, let me help you up." Lucius reached for Tahlia, pulling her to her feet, and then his arms came around to embrace her as they'd done several times before. "I'm going to kill that little brother of mine, and right after I got him back no less."

"Don't," Tahlia cried yet again against Lucius's chest. She couldn't believe she was back here again. Not after Maximus almost died. In her worst nightmare, she'd never thought he'd turn his back on her, but he had. She lifted her head to look up at him. "He's made his feelings perfectly clear where I'm concerned. He doesn't want me, so—so I'm going to leave. Go home and get on with my life."

She started to move away from Lucius, but he touched her arm. "Tahlia. Don't leave. He's not in his right state. Maybe that surgery scrambled his brain somehow. He doesn't know what he's doing. He couldn't. Because if he did, he wouldn't let you go."

"He's knows exactly what he's doing, Lucius. You'll have to learn to accept that Maximus is somewhat of a prick. I have." Then as much as it hurt, she walked down the hall and away from Maximus, the love of her life.

"You stupid jerk!" Lucius barged into Maximus's room, startling him out of the haze of guilt he already felt for sending Tahlia away.

Lucius stabbed his finger in Maximus's direction several times. "You—you—you idiot!" he roared.

"What the hell?" Maximus yelled, covering his ears. "You do realize I'm in the hospital recovering from surgery." His head was still hurting something fierce, and none of the medications they'd given him had worked.

"Don't you dare go pulling the sick card," Lucius

said. "I've been talking to the doctor, and you're going to make a full recovery."

"That must really be upsetting news for you," Maximus responded with a snort. "I'm sure you'd much rather I'd disappear altogether."

"Jesus Christ, Max!" Lucius spun away from him for several moments. He was silent, and Max wondered what he was thinking. When he spun around, he said, "Can't you let up for a second?"

"Why?"

"Don't you get it?"

"Get what?"

"I don't hate you!" Lucius yelled, throwing his hands up in the air. At his words, Maximus was quiet. "I never have."

"Of course you do," Maximus said. "I was the son who grew up with Arthur as a father. I had everything in life handed to me on a silver platter, while you've had to struggle until you achieved success all on your own."

"So what? I've had it no harder than any other person out there," Lucius responded. "At least I had my grandmother and my friend Adam. And my mother occasionally, but she was too busy living her life and refusing to tell me who my father was. That's beside the point, Maximus. Why are *you* so angry? You'd think I would be. I'm the son he didn't acknowledge."

"You think you're the only one with a right to be angry?" Maximus asked, pressing the bed forward so he could sit upright even though his head felt like it was splitting into two. "Well, guess what, big brother. It finally occurred to me why I never had my father's love."

"Why is that?"

"Because I was always the stand-in for the son he really wanted. You. And despite everything I did, no matter how hard I worked, or how much I achieved, it was never good enough for Arthur Knight, because I could never be you, Lucius. So there. That's why I'm angry."

"Maximus." Lucius pulled up the chair that Tahlia had left closer to the bed. "What has that anger gotten you, huh? You've just let one of the best women I've ever met, other than Naomi, walk out." He pointed to the door. "And the only thing I can think of, other than you've lost your mind, is that you don't think you deserve her."

"You have no idea what you're talking about."

Lucius stared at him, and it was as if he could read Maximus's mind. "I think I do. Tahlia and her love for you has you running scared. And I get it, okay? I was scared, too, when I realized I loved Naomi, but I'm telling you, bro, having a woman like Tahlia in your life is the best kind of medicine you'll ever need."

The two men looked at each other, assessing the other. It was Maximus who finally spoke. "Why are you involving yourself in my personal life anyway? This is none of your concern. What's it to you if I'm alone or not?"

"I'm here because I *care*," Lucius stated evenly. "And I want you to be happy, same as me."

"Why? Why should you?"

"Because you're my brother." Lucius pounded his chest. "And that means something to me. I don't know what it means to you, but I grew up alone with no one other than Grandma, and I always wanted a little brother. And when I learned about you at the hospital, I wanted to go to you then, even when my world was shattering around me, and pull you into a hug and tell you everything was going to be all right because that's what a big brother does. But you looked at me with such scorn that I left."

Maximus remembered that night. The night when the world he'd always thought he'd known came crashing down, too. It'd been when he learned his father was a liar, a cheat and an all-around jerk. He'd seen Lucius and the stunned look on his face when he'd learned Arthur was their father. And his heart had gone out to him because he had no idea that he'd actually dodged a bullet. Arthur Knight had been a terrible father.

"You're right," Maximus said. "I was upset. And disillusioned. I'd always looked up to our father. That night I'd realized he was just a man. A fallible man with his own faults."

Lucius nodded. "We all are human, but the key is to learn from our mistakes and take a different path. Just because Arthur wasn't capable of loving you doesn't mean you're the same, Maximus. You can be a better man than him. I know you can be."

Maximus looked at Lucius, truly looked at him. And staring back at him for the first time in his life was someone who believed in him.

His brother.

"It's too late, Lucius," Maximus said, shaking his head. "I hurt Tahlia just now. There's no way she's coming back for more of the same. She told me she loved me, and I said thank you. I ruined everything."

"No, you haven't," Lucius stated emphatically. "While you were gone, we took care of Knight Shipping for you. We got to know each other, and I've never seen a woman more in love than Tahlia is with you. You can still fix this. It's never too late."

"I hope you're right," Maximus replied. He'd hurt Tahlia when he hadn't meant to. He just hadn't known how to love her, but having Lucius here to talk had helped. Helped him see that he was capable of much more if he was only willing to go out on the ledge and jump.

And for Tahlia he would.

Chapter 16

"Man, am I glad to see you," Griffin said when he visited the hospital later that afternoon. He leaned forward on the hospital bed to give Maximus a hug and took a seat in the chair across from him.

"About as happy as I am to see you," Maximus said, sitting up in his bed. "I missed you, Griff. Being out on that boat with a seventy-year-old man was starting to get lonesome."

Griffin shrugged. "You're the one who went on a self-imposed exile and kept all of us at arm's length, but let's not talk about that. How are you feeling?"

"Like crap," Maximus answered honestly. "My head is killing me. The doctor was here earlier and told me that's to be expected."

"Any complications from the surgery?"

Maximus shook his head. "No, the doctor said I should make a full recovery."

"Darn." Griffin snapped his fingers. "I was hoping to get that autographed baseball collection you have."

Maximus chuckled, but when he did, it made his

head hurt, and he rubbed his temples to ease the sharp pain from the laughter.

"Are you sure you're up for a visit?" Griffin asked, starting to rise from his seat. "I can always come back."

"For you, yes. And please stay." He patted the bed, indicating Griffin should sit down. "We haven't seen each other in a couple of months. Catch me up on what's going on with you. I could use the distraction."

Griffin's forehead creased. "I don't understand. Tahlia was here for days when you were injured and after the surgery. Even your brother, Lucius, was here causing a ruckus to make sure you got the best care. I just assumed circumstances had changed."

"They have, sort of," Maximus responded.

"Explain," Griffin said, folding his arms across his chest.

"Lucius and I are going to make an effort at this whole brother thing."

Maximus couldn't help but notice the wide grin that split across Griffin's dark features.

"That's great news, Max. I was hoping that would be the outcome. And Tahlia?"

"Ah...there's where I have a problem." He sighed as he remembered their encounter and how upset Tahlia had been. "I royally screwed up, Griff, and I'm going to have to do some serious damage control to get her back."

Griffin frowned. "What could you have possibly done from your hospital bed?"

"Push her away. She told me she loved me, and I knew she wanted me to say it back. And I wanted to say those words back to her, but I didn't. Instead, I told her there was too much water under the bridge between us and that we'd never work."

"You idiot!" Griffin rose from the chair he was sitting in and began pacing the floor. "After that woman stood by your side? How could you?"

"Please don't read me the riot act, okay? Lucius already did that. I know I have to fix things. And I will. As soon as I get out of here."

Griffin rolled his eyes upward. "You're on thin ice, my friend. If Tahlia gives you another chance, I would suggest you thank your lucky stars because you're not going to find someone who loves and cares for you more."

Maximus smiled. "Yes, I know that, and I promise you when I get out of here, I'm going to rectify the situation. I promise you. I will get Tahlia back."

"Do you really think you can let him go?" Kaitlynn asked Tahlia when she came on Saturday to help Kaitlynn pack boxes. She had helped Kaitlynn with the security deposit and first month's rent to move into a brand-new apartment complex with all the amenities, such as a fitness center and coffee bar. It was the least she could do since being owner of the gallery and a shareholder at Knight Shipping had given her extra cash in her bank account.

"I have no choice," Tahlia said. "Maximus rejected me, Kaitlynn. After I told him that I was at fault, too, and could have supported him instead of standing on my soap box and telling him about Arthur's feelings and wishes." She stopped putting tape on a box long enough to look at her sister. "I sat in front of him, face-to-face, and I told him that I missed him and that his accident had made me see that I couldn't go another minute without telling him how I feel, that I loved him. And you want to know what he said?"

"What?" Kaitlynn asked.

"He said, thank you. Thank you!" Tahlia repeated the words she still couldn't believe she'd heard, even though he'd said them days ago. "He acted as if I'd just given him flowers and a get-well card at the hospital, for Christ's sake. I told him I loved him."

"And you expected him to say it back?"

"I hoped," Tahlia responded with a shrug. "But at the very least, he could have said he cares about me. All I got was he missed me. Most likely he missed all the sex he was getting on the regular."

"It was like that, huh?"

Tahlia blushed and continued taping the box. "We had a very active sex life." But gosh, it seemed like that was decades ago when it had been only less than three months. Being with Maximus had been everything she'd ever imagined it would be. Her body had recognized being with his as if she'd come home, and now it craved his. But she'd have to get used to the fact that they would never be together again in any capacity except at board meetings.

That was when it hit her. And she stopped dead in her tracks.

"What?" Kaitlynn looked at her. "What is it, Tahlia? You look like you've been hit with some sort of revelation."

Tahlia nodded. "That's because I have." Why hadn't it occurred to her before? Maximus saw the shares of Knight Shipping as a stumbling block between them. He'd said so when they'd first broken up, when he'd accused her of not believing in him, of not supporting him and taking his side.

Maybe, just maybe, she had the key after all to salvage what was left of their relationship, if there was one. It was a risky move, but she had to try because if she didn't, she'd always wonder what if. She'd always wonder if they could have survived the drama if only she'd taken the chance.

"I'm glad to be getting out of here," Maximus said as he rose from the hospital bed and sat down in the wheelchair the nurse held for him.

"You and me both," his mother said from behind him. "I practically had to fight that brother of yours over which of us would be coming to pick you up and drive you home."

"Oh, yeah?" Maximus asked, laughing. It had surprised him, too, at the active role Lucius was now taking in his life. Ever since their talk a week ago, he'd made his presence known by visiting Maximus every day in the hospital. They would talk for hours about growing up, school, sports and, of course, women. They'd even played cards, and Lucius had taught him how to play poker. And slowly, Maximus was beginning to see the makings of a relationship with his brother.

"Yes," his mother harrumphed. "It was only when I'd agreed to have him and Naomi over for dinner that he'd finally relented."

Maximus glanced up at his mother. "Thank you. It means a lot to me that you're making an effort where Lucius is concerned."

She patted his shoulder, and then the nurse began wheeling him out of the room and toward the elevator. "Lucius and Naomi, yes, but his mother will never be welcomed in my home again."

He reached for his mother's hand and squeezed. "That's understandable. And I'm sure Lucius will understand. The only reason you allowed her the first time after the reading of the will was at my bequest."

"Thank you, darling," his mother replied. "And Naomi, she's such a lovely girl. Lucius is very lucky to have her."

Maximus gave her a sideward glance. "Yes, he is." Naomi had brought him a lovely get-well basket full of products from her men's line to make sure his stay at the hospital was more comfortable. He couldn't ask for a better sister-in-law.

"Makes me think of Tahlia and what a great addition she would be to the family."

"Matchmaking again, mother?"

"Me?" She touched her chest. "Never. You've told me time and time again to stay out of your love life. I was merely reminding you that Tahlia was at your bedside day and night when you were injured until you woke up."

"I know that." Lying in his hospital bed, he'd thought of nothing else but how he could get Tahlia back. What he could do to convince her to give him another chance. She certainly didn't have to give him one, not after he'd done the exact same thing his father had done to him. He'd thrown her love for him back in her face.

It was why he waited. He needed time, not only to heal, but to think of something grand. When he'd told Lucius of his idea, Lucius had given him some solid advice. *Speak from your heart.*

Would that be enough? Would Tahlia hear him when he told her he loved her and never wanted to live without her?

"I don't appreciate being summoned to meet you," Kaitlynn Armstrong said when Maximus arrived in a limousine to pick her up at her apartment complex at the beginning of the week.

"I'm sure you don't," Maximus responded. "I know I can't be your favorite person right now."

"That's right," Kaitlynn said. Her brown eyes turned to daggers when they looked at him. "You hurt Tahlia deeply *twice*. So I'm not sure what else you want, Maximus. It wasn't enough to have her madly and deeply in love with you?"

"Listen, Kaitlynn—"

"No, you listen. I've watched my sister pine for you for a year. And when she finally got a chance to meet you, she jumped right in with both feet and fell hard for you, Maximus Xavier Knight. While you, on the other hand, were only using her for your own agenda. It was despicable."

"You're right, Kat," he replied. "May I call you Kat?" He remembered Tahlia always used the nickname around her.

"Kat is for my friends, and I don't think you're one of them anymore."

Maximus smiled. She was tough, and he deserved it. "Maybe I can be, which is why I called you. I need your help."

"My help? To get my sister back? You must be joking."

"I'm not. You're right. I don't deserve Tahlia. I did have an ulterior motive when we began seeing each other, but all of that changed the more I got to know your sister. The more time we spent together, the deeper I fell in love with her."

Kaitlynn stared back at him. "Then why did you let her go, you big oaf!" She smacked his shoulder hard with her hand. "She stayed by your side in the hospital,

admitted her shortcomings, and you still let her walk
out that door."

"Because I'm an idiot!" Maximus said. "A complete
and utter fool, but a fool who loves your sister. And
you're right. I want her back, and I need your help to
do it."

"I don't know how to help you. You're on your own."
She shrugged.

"Oh, you can help me," Maximus said, stepping out
of the limousine that had come to a halt. "Come inside
and let me show you how." He held his hand out to her.

Kaitlynn glanced at him in bewilderment, as she
clearly hadn't noticed the car had stopped. But when she
exited the vehicle and saw their destination, she smiled
at him. "You sly, sly devil. You really are as smart as
they say you are."

Tahlia drove up to the Knight estate. Lucius had
called her to inform her, *if she was interested*, that Maximus had been released from the hospital days ago. He
knew darn well that she was interested.

Her love for his brother hadn't suddenly flown the
coop in a week's time. But she did have news for Lucius. News he hadn't exactly been shocked to hear. It
had taken her a few days to finalize the details, but
she'd made it happen, and surprisingly he hadn't tried to
change her mind or talk her out of it. Not that he could.
She was adamant in her decision, and no one was going
to talk her out of it.

She'd expected more of a reaction from him, but instead of trying to change her mind, Lucius had wished
her good luck and said he hoped his brother finally saw
the light, which was that she was a woman worth hang-
ing on to. Tahlia thought so.

And so she'd taken a leap of faith by coming here. Maximus could very well turn her away and refuse to see her, but she was hoping against hope that he wouldn't turn her away.

Parking her VW Bug, she exited and headed for the large solid oak door of the Knight estate. She was greeted several moments later by a uniformed butler.

"Tahlia Armstrong," she told him. "I'm here to see—"

"Maximus," he said before she could finish. "I will fetch him for you. Please follow me into the sitting room."

He led her into a large room.

"Thank you," she said, taking a seat on a wingback chair.

"Can I get you any refreshments?" the butler inquired.

"No, that won't be necessary. I won't be staying long," Tahlia replied.

"That's too bad," Maximus said from the doorway. "Because I was hoping you'd stay awhile."

Tahlia's breath caught in her throat at the sight of him. He was *all right*. He was standing there looking like he'd just stepped out of a fashion magazine instead of a hospital bed. He wore jeans and a V-neck sweater, and he'd never looked more handsome to Tahlia. She swallowed the lump in her throat.

She'd come here with a purpose and she just had to get to it, but Maximus didn't seem to be in any hurry. Instead, he looked at his butler and said, "Can you bring us a pot of tea? Maybe chamomile? You'd like that, right?"

Tahlia smiled. He remembered that she liked chamomile tea and that it calmed her nerves. "Yes, that'll be fine."

The butler left the room, and Maximus took a seat across from Tahlia on the opposite wingback chair.

"I'm glad to see that you're looking well," Tahlia started. "How are you feeling?"

"I'm doing well," he responded. "Still a little weak and not where I'd like to be, but the doctor said that's normal after a couple of weeks in the hospital. He said once I exercise my muscles again that I'll be right as rain."

"Good, good." Tahlia nodded. "So…" Her words trailed off as she tried to figure out how to start the conversation. She'd never had trouble conversing with him, but this time was different. This time their entire relationship was on the line.

"So, I'm happy you came to see me."

Her brows drew together in confusion. "You are?"

He nodded. "I didn't like how I ended our last meeting."

"Neither did I," Tahlia said. "It was unpleasant, to say the least, but it's over and done with." She sat up more firmly in her chair. "It's actually why I'm here."

"Is that so?" Maximus scooted closer to the edge of the seat, and in so doing, their knees touched. The tiny action caused both of them to look up at each other.

Tahlia was surprised at what she saw there. Was that lust lurking in his eyes? Or was she imagining what she wanted to see there because she'd been unable to get Maximus out of her mind and her subconscious was manifesting itself?

She exhaled and tried again. "Yes. I thought you might want this." She reached inside her purse for the manila envelope and handed it to Maximus.

"What's this?"

"Open it. It's something you've always wanted."

Maximus was afraid to open the envelope and stared at it in his hands. What could Tahlia possibly be giving to him? And then it hit him, the only thing she could do to prove she believed in him.

He looked at her, and the depth of emotion on her face told him he was right. This had cost her, but she was doing it because she loved him and because she believed in him.

He handed her the envelope back. "I don't want this."

She frowned. "Why not? You haven't even opened it. You don't even know what's inside."

"I don't have to open it because I know what it says."

The butler returned, breaking the moment, and set the tray with the teapot, cups and cream and sugar in front of them on the settee. He went to pour it, but Maximus stopped him. "Thank you, I've got it."

Maximus reached for the teapot and began pouring, stalling for time as he prepared for the biggest speech of his life. The moment was here. Tahlia had come to him yet again, offering him everything she had in the hopes that this time he wouldn't reject her love.

He wouldn't make that mistake twice.

Maximus handed her the teacup and saucer and watched as she brought it to her delectable lips. And despite his injuries, his shaft sprung to life.

When she was finished sipping, she set the cup down on the settee. "Aren't you having any?"

He shook his head. He probably should have some tea to calm his nerves. He'd never told a woman he loved her before, so this was certainly a first.

"Tahlia…" he began, but she interrupted.

"Why won't you open that envelope?" she asked, inclining her head to the envelope sitting on the settee.

"I don't need to," he responded. "It says that you've signed your two percent share in Knight Shipping over to me."

Her eyes grew large in surprise. "H-how did you know? Did Lucius say something to you?"

Maximus chuckled. "So my brother knew you were going to do this and he let you?"

"Like he could stop me," Tahlia replied with a snort. "It's my stock to do with as I please, and I'm choosing to give it to you because it's rightfully yours and because it's what you deserve. Knight Shipping should have been yours to begin with. You earned it, but instead your father chose otherwise. And I'm here to tell you he was wrong, Maximus. He should have chosen you, because I do. And I always choose you each and every time."

"Oh, God, Tahlia." Maximus fell to his knees in front of her and clutched at her legs. "I don't deserve you. I never have, but I'm so glad you're here and that you'd do this *for me*."

Tahlia's hands grasped both sides of his face, and Maximus thought he'd died and gone to heaven just to have her touch him again. How he'd longed for her! "I'd do anything for you," she said, "even come here again, not knowing how you'd react and…and—" Her words got choked from emotion, and she stopped, dropping her hands from his face.

"Not knowing if I'd reject your love again," he finished, glancing up at her warily.

She nodded as fresh tears formed in her eyes.

"I won't," Maximus said, shaking his head. "I won't ever again."

"You won't?" Her voice was hesitant and unsure.

He couldn't put his feelings into words as relief surged through him. Tahlia was one in a million. She was without guile and had every reason to hate him, to never want to see him again, but instead she'd come here with her heart in her hands asking for his love yet again. He wouldn't fail her.

Summoning all the courage he'd ever had, Maximus took her hands in his and raised them to his lips. He couldn't resist the forces any longer. She'd unlocked the door to his heart, a door he'd kept hidden because of his father, but she'd transformed him and set him free.

"I love you, Tahlia," Maximus said simply, remembering Lucius's words to speak from the heart. "And I'm sorry for everything. For foolishly thinking that I could seduce you into my way of thinking to vote for me when it was you who was seducing me with your every look, your every action and your every kiss."

Tears shone in Tahlia's eyes at his words, and Maximus was thankful that she wasn't pulling away from him. Instead, she was clutching his hand to her heart, and Maximus's heart swelled with love. He hadn't lost her!

"You're my every dream come true, Tahlia. You're the dream I didn't even know I was looking for, but I am so happy that I found you. I was a scared man before you came into my life. Afraid of love because I'd been rejected by my father so many times."

"I know that, sweetheart." She whispered the endearment.

"I was so afraid to let you in because I was afraid of being rejected, but what did I do? I did the same thing to you that my father did to me. In the hospital, I rejected your love even though you'd been there for me in my time of need, and I'm not sure if I'll ever truly forgive myself for hurting you that way. But I promise you that I will spend my every waking minute trying, trying to be the best man that I can be for you, the woman I love."

"Oh, Maximus!" she cried and threw her arms around his neck and began planting kisses on his neck and ears, but he pulled away.

"Wait, sweetheart. I'm not done yet."

"You're not? I thought that was really, really good," she said. "Can't you just stop there?"

"No." He shook his head. "Because there's so much more I have to say."

"Like what?"

"That you didn't have to give me your stock," Maximus said, glancing down at the manila envelope that sat on the table.

"Of course I did. I wanted to show you that I just want you. And only you. None of it, any of it, means a thing without you in my life."

"And you mean more to me than Knight Shipping. So much more. Do you have any idea how much you've enriched my life?" he asked. "You've helped bridge the gap between me and Lucius."

"I have?"

"Yes, we've been talking since I've been in the hospital, and I have to admit, I kind of like having an older brother. Someone to bounce ideas off of. And it's why I can't let you give away what's rightfully half his."

"But he doesn't want Knight Shipping," Tahlia said. "He just wants you to be happy."

Maximus grinned and playfully tapped her nose. "There you go again, ever the optimist."

She shrugged. "What can I say? It's who I am."

Maximus swung her into his arms, causing them

both to fall onto the floor. Tahlia ended up on the rug with Maximus hovering over her. He loved looking at her and knew he'd never tire of it. So he took his fill now. Tahlia was all he would ever need. "And I love who you are," he said, lowering his head until his lips were mere inches from hers. "Matter of fact, I love everything about you."

And then he did the one thing he'd wanted most, the one thing he'd missed over the last few months. Maximus finally kissed Tahlia.

Chapter 17

A kiss had never been sweeter to Tahlia than the one Maximus bestowed on her after he'd just professed his love to her. She'd taken a risk coming to the estate today, and it had paid off. Maximus now held her in his arms on the throw rug in his family's sitting room as he kissed her gently at first, stroking her hair.

Tahlia cried out in disappointment. She wanted more. It didn't help that the scent of his cologne was teasing her senses, and it made every part of Tahlia's body tingle, especially when she felt the jut of his erection in his jeans. Her nipples thrust toward him through the confines of her blouse, desperate for his touch. They hadn't been together in so long; she didn't want to wait a moment longer.

Tahlia began writhing beneath him even more so when he dipped his head and licked at the seams of her mouth, seeking entry. She parted her already moistened lips, and his tongue darted inside, possessively mating with hers until she was going mad for him. Her senses were roaring to new heights, and she arched into him for greater contact and was rewarded when she felt the hard ridge of his manhood pushing against her pelvis. But Maximus stopped her.

"We should, uh, take this to my room," he murmured huskily.

That was when Tahlia realized that they were still on the throw in the middle of his family's sitting room. He had aroused her to fever pitch, making her forget their location. She blushed beet red. "Yes, of course."

They left everything in the room, including her purse, exactly where it was, and she took the hand Maximus offered her and let him lead her to his bedroom. It was up a flight of stairs and down the hall, heightening the anticipation of finally being with Maximus after so long without him.

When they finally made it inside the room, Maximus closed and locked the door. Then they began peeling their clothes off, eager to feel the friction of body against naked body.

"I've looked forward to this moment for so long," Tahlia said as they met on the bed, and he slid down on top of her.

"As have I." Then he claimed her mouth with a hot, hungry kiss. Tahlia moaned as he kissed her with skilled mastery. Her entire body trembled with every thrust of his tongue inside her mouth. His tongue invaded hers, and all Tahlia could do was take, take more of him as he went deeper, giving her everything. And when his lips left hers to nip at her earlobe and then glide to her neck and throat, molten heat began to pool between her thighs.

Maximus had always made her feel this way, this hot, this aroused with him and only him. Then his hand slipped underneath her and downward to cup her backside, bringing his arousal against her belly and rubbing her *there* with his engorged tip. Tahlia wanted to drag him inside her to have every inch of his skin imprinted on her. She writhed in his hold, eager for him to reach her slit, but instead of driving into her, he slid her up and down the steel of his erection with slow, leisurely strokes.

"Enough of the foreplay," Tahlia whimpered. "Please... take me."

"Not yet," Maximus said and began molding and massaging her breasts before dipping his head to sample one and then the other. At the graze of his tongue, licking and swirling her breasts, corkscrews of ecstasy went through Tahlia, and she was forced to take a sharp breath.

But he continued his onslaught of her senses when his hands delved between her thighs and touched her exactly where she wanted him to, dipping and withdrawing, making her pant his name as he stoked the fire deep within her. She opened her legs wider to give him better access. And he took it, moving down her body.

His hands were no longer possessing. It was his mouth at her slick, hot core, milking every ounce of her satisfaction as he used his tongue and teeth to suckle her. She whimpered and keened as he licked his way in and out of her, pleading for him to end her agony as she bucked helplessly beneath his lashing tongue.

She was sweaty and delirious when she finally saw him pause long enough to put on a condom, and then he was back between her thighs, thrusting into her. He plunged inside her, into the very depths of her, then he withdrew and plunged in deeper until he was all the way inside her. Then he began moving, slowly, then faster and faster until she convulsed and shattered around him. Maximus's roar came next, and he stiffened in her arms, but he didn't stop ramming into her until her body gave way again and she shattered into a million pieces.

Maximus gathered Tahlia's exhausted and shaking body into his arms. He loved her so much and with everything in him. What they'd shared just now was more than physical. It transcended anything he'd ever felt. Time and space ceased to exist. And he knew he never wanted to let her go. He loved her.

When Tahlia finally began to stir, he found she was still awake. "Hello, beautiful." He stroked her cheek.

"Did I pass out?" she asked in disbelief.

He laughed. "Uh, something like that."

She poked him in the ribs. "Don't tease me. You just wore me out. I wasn't prepared for your exuberance."

Maximus thought about how he reveled in the taste of her sweet stickiness when he'd been between her thighs. Her sighs of pleasure as he'd licked her and she'd pleaded with him to take her. He liked that she gave herself so completely to him, but there was one final thing he hadn't done.

Maximus slid from the bed and reached for the nightstand drawer.

Tahlia saw his actions and held his hand. "Oh, no you don't, mister. My highly sensitized flesh needs time to recover."

He chuckled to himself. She thought he was reaching for another condom; he wasn't. Instead, he reached for the ring box he'd purchased yesterday, thanks to a little help from Kaitlynn, Tahlia's sister. After leaving the hospital, he'd called her and picked her up. He needed assistance because he wasn't sure what ring Tahlia might like. At first, Kaitlynn hadn't been too keen to meet up with the man who'd broken her sister's heart, but when he'd told her just how much he loved Tahlia and that he would make things right, she'd agreed. And they'd found a beautiful six-carat princess-cut diamond ring.

"Tahlia." Maximus kneeled at the bedside. "I know this might seem sudden to you since we're just getting back together, but you were right about something. Having a near-death experience changes you. And it changed me. It made me see life is short, and I don't want to miss a single minute of being with you." He opened the ring box. "Tahlia Armstrong, will you do me the honor of being my wife? Will you marry me?

"Wh-what?" Tahlia's eyes grew large with wonder. "You want to marry me?"

He nodded. "I was so lonely until you came into my life, but you've brightened up my whole world. You've changed my life, Tahlia, and I'm the better for it. So I want us to last a lifetime. Please—say you'll marry me."

Tears streamed down Tahlia's cheeks as she looked at him and nodded. "You've changed my life, too, Maximus. You've enriched it with your love and your encouragement. So yes, I'll marry you."

Maximus clutched her shoulders and kissed her. His lips parted hers with bold assurance, and his tongue slid firmly between them to explore her with an eroticism that left her trembling. "You've made me the happiest man alive, Tahlia." Then he slipped the diamond ring onto her finger.

"And I'm the happiest woman alive," Tahlia said. Then she pulled him into her embrace as she whispered, "Now I'm ready for round two."

Epilogue

"I never thought I'd see the day that Maximus and Lucius would be running Knight Shipping together," Tahlia said as she and Naomi set the table at Maximus's penthouse. Lucius and Naomi were joining them for dinner because she and Maximus had just returned from their honeymoon in Saint Bart's.

They'd had their wedding on the Knight estate on the great lawn surrounded by family and friends. Her mother had walked Tahlia down the aisle, and Kaitlynn and Griffin had been maid of honor and best man. Lucius had been groomsman and Naomi bridesmaid, along with her coworker, Faith. It had been a spectacular day, one that Tahlia would never forget.

"Neither did I," Naomi said. "That was no small feat you accomplished, sister-in-law."

Tahlia turned and stared at her husband while he and Lucius grilled steaks on the grill on the balcony outside. "I didn't do it alone. It took both of our strong, yet very powerful husbands to put in the work."

"True, but you were the catalyst."

"No." Tahlia shook her head. "In his own weird way,

it was their father, Arthur," Tahlia said. "Though I don't think even he could have envisioned this."

Tahlia smiled as the two brothers sparred over who was the better grill master and drank their beers.

"How was the honeymoon?" Naomi queried as she played with her curly fro. Tahlia wished she was like her sister-in-law and could rock the natural look.

"Oh, Saint Bart's was amazing," Tahlia said, "and somewhat exhausting. Your brother-in-law was insatiable."

Naomi giggled. "It must run in the family."

Later, when both couples were gathered at the table, Maximus opened a bottle of wine and began pouring each of them a glass.

"None for me," Naomi said, placing her hand over the rim of the wineglass.

"Are you feeling all right?" Maximus inquired as the foursome usually drank quite frequently together as they each had a love of wine bars.

Naomi beamed from across the table, and Tahlia instantly knew the truth. "I'm feeling fine." She patted her flat belly. "I'm just eating for two now, so it's best I avoid alcoholic substances for the next six months."

Maximus's eyes grew large, and he reached across the table and pulled Lucius into a one-armed hug. "Congratulations, bro. And you, too, Naomi." He looked at his sister-in-law. "This is wonderful news. I'm going to be an uncle."

"That's right." Lucius grinned from ear to ear. "My baby is having a baby."

"Aw, honey." Naomi smiled at his sweet words.

"Soon it'll be your turn, Max," Lucius stated. "You mark my words."

Maximus chuckled as he looked across the table at his gorgeous wife. "Well, it certainly won't be for lack of trying on my part. I kept Tahlia flat on her back for most of our honeymoon."

"Maximus Xavier Knight!" Tahlia blushed from across the table.

He grinned mischievously. "Sorry, babe." But deep down, he wasn't sorry. He couldn't wait for the day when Tahlia told him she was pregnant.

He told her so later that evening, after Lucius and Naomi had gone and it was just the two of them staring out at the Los Angeles skyline on the balcony of the penthouse.

"You don't want to wait?" Tahlia asked, glancing behind her. Her back was to him, and Maximus had circled his arms around her middle. "I'd think you'd want me all to yourself." She could feel the bulge in his pants. Her husband had a voracious appetite for her.

"I do," Maximus whispered, nuzzling her neck and planting soft kisses there. "But I can't wait to see your belly swollen with my child."

Tahlia spun around in his arms to face him. Her hands stroked the sides of his face as she peered intently into his dark eyes. "And I can't wait to be the mother of your children."

And she sealed her wish with a kiss.

* * * * *

If you enjoyed this enticing story,
check out more of Yahrah St. John's titles:

HEAT WAVE OF DESIRE
CAPPUCCINO KISSES
TAMING HER TYCOON
MIAMI AFTER HOURS

Available now from Harlequin Kimani Romance!

KIMANI™
ROMANCE

COMING NEXT MONTH
Available November 21, 2017

#549 SEDUCED BY THE TYCOON AT CHRISTMAS
The Morretti Millionaires • by Pamela Yaye
Italy's most powerful businessman, Romeo Morretti, spends his days brokering multimillion-dollar deals, but an encounter with Zoe Smith sends his life in a new direction. When secrets threaten their passionate bond, Romeo must fight to clear his name before they can share a future under the mistletoe.

#550 A LOVE LIKE THIS
Sapphire Shores • by Kianna Alexander
All action star Devon Granger wants for Christmas is a peaceful escape to his hometown. How is he to rest with Hadley Monroe tending to his every need? And when the media descends on the beachfront community, their dreams of ringing in the New Year together could be out of their grasp…

#551 AN UNEXPECTED HOLIDAY GIFT
The Kingsleys of Texas • by Martha Kennerson
When a scuffle leads to community service, basketball star Keylan "KJ" Kingsley opts to devote his hours to his family's foundation. Soon he plunges into a relationship with charity executive Mia Ramirez. When KJ returns to the court, will his celebrity status risk the family that could be theirs by Christmas?

#552 DESIRE IN A KISS
The Chandler Legacy • by Nicki Night
On impulse, heir to a food empire Christian Chandler creates a fake dating profile and quickly connects with petite powerhouse Serenity Williams. She's smart, down-to-earth and ignites his fantasies from their first encounter. But how can he admit the truth to a woman for whom honesty is everything?

Get 2 Free Books,
Plus 2 Free Gifts—
just for trying the Reader Service!

LOVE
Harlequin
romance?

Join our Harlequin community to share your thoughts and connect with other romance readers!

Be the first to find out about promotions, news, and exclusive content!

Sign up for the Harlequin e-newsletter and download a free book from any series at

www.TryHarlequin.com

Want to give in to temptation with
steamy tales of irresistible desire?

Check out **Harlequin® Presents®,
Harlequin® Desire** and
Harlequin® Kimani™ Romance books!

New books available every month!

Looking for inspiration in tales
of hope, faith and heartfelt romance?

Check out **Love Inspired**®,
Love Inspired® **Suspense** and
Love Inspired® **Historical** books!

New books available every month!

CONNECT WITH US AT:

www.LoveInspired.com

Harlequin.com/Community

 Facebook.com/LoveInspiredBooks

 Twitter.com/LoveInspiredBooks

www.ReaderService.com

Love Inspired®

Reward the book lover in you!

Earn points from all your Harlequin book purchases from wherever you shop.

Turn your points into *FREE BOOKS* of your choice
OR
EXCLUSIVE GIFTS from your favorite authors or series.

Join for FREE today at
www.HarlequinMyRewards.com.

Harlequin My Rewards is a free program (no fees) without any commitments or obligations.

MYR17